A KILLER'S LOVE SERIES BOOK FIVE

JENNIFER IVY

Copyright © 2025 by Jennifer Ivy

All rights reserved.

No part of this book may be reproduced in any form or by any electronic or mechanical means, including information storage and retrieval systems, without written permission from the author, except for the use of brief quotations in a book review.

This is a work of fiction.

Edited by editing4Indies

Cover designed by Cormar Covers

 Formatted with Vellum

Dedication

For everyone that has joined me on this journey so far and read through my first series.
Thank you.

TRIGGER WARNINGS

This book is a Dark Romance, and as such may contain subject matters, content, or events that you may find disturbing.

This includes but is not limited to:

Dubious Consent (Dubcon)

Non Consent (Noncon)

Doctor/Patient Relationship

Age Gap

Breeding Kink

Loss of a Child/Miscarriage

Car Accident

Somnophilia

Graphic descriptions of Violence, Torture, and Murder.

A KILLER'S LOVE SERIES BOOK FIVE

JENNIFER IVY

CHAPTER ONE

Shelby

"Want to tell me what happened?" I whisper.

Sam shakes her head. Closing her eyes, she wipes at the wetness on her lashes with the heel of her hands, pushing the blond hair out of her face.

I open my mouth but say nothing. She's been my best friend since high school, and I know when to back off.

Whatever happened between her and her brother is staying between them.

My phone chimes on the arm of the sofa next to my hand.

I take that back.

Kaleb's name flashes on the screen.

"It's him," I tell her.

"Ignore it."

But we both know I can't. He'll just call again . . . and again. I shrug a quick sorry, earning an eye roll.

"Hey, Kaleb," I greet, trying to keep it light.

"Hi, sweetpea, is she with you?"

Seems I'm not the only one putting on a front. I've known this man just as long as his sister. He's pissed. Like mad, mad.

"Who?" I ask. God loves a tryer.

"Give Samantha the phone," he demands dryly.

"You're on speaker," I murmur.

Samantha's eyes widen. I wave my hand. What did she expect me to do?

"I've been calling and texting you."

I push the cell close to the blonde when she doesn't answer him.

Finally, she drags out, "Don't have my phone."

"We've talked about this, Samantha."

I imagine Kaleb with his eyes closed, praying for patience, and cringe.

"You're not my fucking dad," Sam snaps.

My mouth forms a small O. She should not have said that. Talk about poking the bear. The man may not be her dad, but he has spent the past few years looking out for her.

For me too. Kaleb was one of the first people to check in on me after my dad passed earlier this year.

My heart squeezes with loss. I miss him. I push out a breath and send the thought with it. If I think about Dad now, I'll cry.

"I noticed. The other night made that particularly clear."

Sam and I gasp, his insinuation clear.

My eyes bulge at his words.

Nooooo way!

Maybe I'm not such a freak thinking that there was something between them after all. I mean, he's not actually her brother, and they are together all the time. But the only thing that happened lately was a home invasion at Kaleb's.

I frown. Horror races through me at the memory of hiding scared in the bathroom. Kaleb killed two men to protect Sam and me on Halloween. Frankly, the man can do no wrong in my eyes. If they want to act on what they've been dancing around for years, I'll be their biggest cheerleader.

Besides, Samantha isn't the only one I love. Kaleb and the rest of the Cromwells are family too.

"What's this I hear about a belated Halloween party?"

He's such a dad.

"None of your business," Sam answers for us.

"Shelby?"

Unlike my best friend, I instantly fold.

"I told you that I don't like Halloween. I invited a few friends over so I wasn't alone, but then the burglaries started happening. Everyone canceled their trick-or-treating plans, so I called off the party."

"So it's canceled? Then why am I hearing about it from Edward's dad?"

3

I look at Sam for help, but she's got nothing.

"Well, it was canceled, but then everyone heard what happened at your house, and they wanted a party to relax. Some of the parents and kids are trick-or-treating today instead, so I thought, why not?" We weren't the only ones worried about the recent break-ins. Now that the culprits are gone, we can all relax. "It's nothing huge, just a few friends, food, and films. More of a movie night," I rush to add.

The line goes quiet, and for a second, I think we've won.

"No alcohol, and make sure you lock up after everyone leaves. I'm sure you'll have fun, but Samantha won't be there."

What? No!

"Yes, I will!" Sam argues.

But I know we've already lost. "Why not?"

"She's grounded," Kaleb answers, ignoring Sam's outrage.

"No, I'm not!"

"Awww, what for?" I moan.

"For not having her phone and being unavailable. Clearly having a word about it wasn't enough."

Not ready to give up, Sam continues to argue, "You can't ground me. I'm not a fucking child, Kaleb."

"Yet you're acting like one. Stop fucking ignoring me."

Clearly, I'm missing something. *What happened between them after the break-in?*

I didn't think Sam's face could get any redder. I was wrong. "Go fuck yourself," she spits.

I may not have a sibling, but I've been around Sam and her brothers long enough to know that this is about to get ugly. My finger stabs the red circle on the screen, ending the call.

My heart stills.

"You hung up," Sam states, just as shocked as I am.

"I know," I whisper. "I didn't mean to."

We stare at each other in silence for a minute before Sam dissolves into laughter, dragging me with her. My hands cover my face.

"He's gonna be so mad."

"I know!" She nods.

"You two would have argued, and it would have gotten worse and worse, and I just thought it was best to you know"—I swipe my hand through the air—"cut it off."

Sam slumps back into the corner of the sofa, all laughter forgotten. "Something needs cutting off."

"Want to talk about it?" I ask again softly.

"No."

"I'm here when you want to," I remind her, nudging her foot with mine as I settle into the other corner of the sofa.

Sam checks the time on her watch. "I should go."

"You're really not coming tonight? Since when do you listen to the word no?" I raise a brow in challenge. She knows I'm right, and her smirk says it.

"It's different this time."

Not wanting to push, I let it go.

"Maybe I should cancel."

"No, don't. I'd feel even worse than I already do. You hate this time of year, so if you want a party, have a party. Besides, even if you cancel now, people will still turn up."

True.

"You ever going to tell me why you hate Halloween? It was your favorite holiday when we were kids."

My blood heats. The past few Halloweens have been . . . different. "Sure." I nod. "Right after you tell me about this thing between you and Kaleb."

"Oh, look at the time," Sam exclaims, glancing at the wrist that doesn't have a watch on.

My laughter booms out. Following her lead, I stand.

At the door, the blonde pulls me in for a tight hug.

"You sure you're going to be okay?"

I nod and open the front door. "Besides, like you said, people will just turn up, so I might as well be here. A few scary movies and a glass of wine might get me out of this funk."

Sam pauses in the open door of her car. "Soon, you, me, a bottle of wine each, and no secrets," she yells over the roof of her car.

Stepping onto the drive, I nod. "Sounds like a plan." *It really does.*

Waving, I watch her reverse out onto the street. Sam returns the gesture before pulling away. I twist quickly when she waves at someone to the right of me.

My cheeks heat at the sight. Dr. Leonard Moore. By far the most attractive man in town, and that's saying something.

Good-looking, hardworking, smart, stern, sweet, and most of all, a devoted father. The man will do anything to make his daughter happy, which explains the costume.

My brows furrow. "What are you?"

His head pulls back, like he can't believe what I just asked. "A Pokémon ball."

My eyes roam his body. Red polo shirt with a thick black belt running through the loops of white dress pants.

Oh!

A smile splits my face.

"Don't you dare laugh." He points.

I hold up my hands. "Never. It's cute." I smile. "Where's Riley?" I ask about his daughter.

"Bathroom." He nods back to his house. Doc's eyes roam over me again. "How are you?" he asks.

"Good." I smile.

"You're staying at Kaleb's again?" he questions, his voice light, but the accusation is loud and clear.

"No, it was just for Halloween." I shrug. "With the break-ins and everything, I didn't want to be here alone."

I watch his cheek twitch at the mention of the holiday.

"You should have stayed with us," he reprimands.

I shift from foot to foot. "I know," I whisper, remembering his previous offer. "I just . . ." I shrug, again. "Sam didn't want to be alone, and I didn't want to be alone. Made sense."

Strong fingers pinch my chin, forcing my gaze to meet his through his black-rimmed glasses. "Next time, you stay with us."

My tongue feels swollen and dry. Unable to talk, I nod.

"At least Kaleb took care of the problem. They ruined Halloween." His face darkens.

I frown at his grumbled words. *Took care of.* As if Kaleb didn't kill two intruders. He's right about one thing, though. They did ruin Halloween.

Did they? I cringe at the thought. Without the break-ins, I would have been home, but I wouldn't have been alone, at least not all night.

I haven't been alone for the past three Halloweens.

One night, once a year, hidden in the darkness of night and sleep, he visits me. Uses me.

Nameless, faceless, he leaves me with no memory of the night before and only his essence between my legs as proof he was ever in my room.

Feeling my cheeks heat, I step back from Leonard.

"At least you get a redo," I point out, gesturing to his costume.

Doc looks at me, confused. "What do you mean?"

"Tonight is this year's Halloween. The kids are trick-or-treating, and the parties are happening later, so it might as well be."

"Tonight is Halloween," he mumbles before his face splits into a smile. "I like it." He nods.

"Shelby!"

We both turn to see a very excited Riley running out of the house. My grin matches her father's.

The little yellow body slams into my legs, fuzzy arms wrapping around my thighs in a tight hug.

"Hi, muffin," I greet. Pulling away, I crouch to return her hug. "You are the cutest Pikachu ever!"

I feel her stiffen at my words. The little girl pulls away, wearing a solemn expression.

"What's wrong?" I look between the six-year-old and her dad.

Riley pushes the hood of her onesie down, leaving little pieces of yellow fuzz behind in her hair.

"I don't want to be cute."

"Oh." I look at her dad.

"Apparently, Max from her class says that you can't get candy if you're not scary. Baby, Daddy already told you it's not true."

Max is a little asshole.

"Not only do you get candy if you're cute but you actually get more," I tell her, but she doesn't look convinced. "In fact, I only dress cute when I trick-or-treat."

"Really?" she asks quietly.

"Mm-hmm." I nod.

"What are you dressing as?"

Shit.

"Well, I don't have anyone to trick-or-treat with, so I'm having a few friends over later instead." *Nice save.* I give myself a mental pat on the back.

"You can share my daddy and come with us."

I melt at her offer. "That's very sweet, muffin." At a loss for an excuse, I look at my neighbor for help.

He doesn't offer any. "You're welcome to join."

With no energy to fight, I raise a brow. "I'd have to change. Give me twenty minutes?"

"Ten," he compromises.

"Fifteen?"

"Twelve."

"Done!" I offer Riley my hand and start hopping toward my house. Giggling, the little girl copies me.

"Eleven minutes!" her dad calls out.

Gasping in fake outrage, I stop abruptly. "Quick, muffin." Bending, I wrap my arm around her small waist and lift, tucking her under my arm like a football. "Run!"

Running into the house with her held tight, we leave a trail of giggles. Closing the front door behind me, I flick the lock. It's become a habit whenever I enter or leave the house for the past three years. A compulsion, not that it ever kept him out.

Carefully, I drop Riley onto my bed.

"Right, muffin. I think I have an old costume somewhere."

Opening my closet, I drag out an old trunk. *Hopefully, something still fits.* Pushing clothes aside, I search for what I'm looking for.

"Think your daddy will give me more time?" I call back to Riley, still digging through the trunk.

"No," a deep voice rumbles.

"Ahh!" I let out a short scream, jumping so hard I knock the trunk. The lid falls, hitting me on the top of my head.

A large hand strokes the back of my hair, while his other hand holds the trunk open.

"Careful," Doc reprimands.

"You scared me. How did you get in?" I glare up at him from my place on the wooden floor.

"The front door."

"I locked it," I whisper.

"Apparently not."

My heart thuds.

"You find something to wear?" he asks, gesturing to the large trunk.

Blinking, I stare at him for a minute.

I did lock it, didn't I?

Silently, I lift the white onesie.

"A snowman?" He smiles.

"I went to a party a couple of years ago, and the theme was *Frozen*."

"Olaf!"

Well, Riley approves. I turn to her dad.

"The best I can do on short notice."

"It's perfect. Riley and I will wait in the living room."

As soon as they're out of sight, my smile drops.

I locked that door.

Didn't I?

CHAPTER TWO

Shelby

"Shelby, look what I got."

Riley runs from the house to the end of the path, joining me on the sidewalk.

Peering into the open tote bag, I grin. "Nice!"

"Next one!" She directs us, running ahead.

"This is fun. Thank you for the invite."

"It is." Doc nods. "So is the sugar high. When she comes down off it, not so much."

"Sounds like a late night for you." I chuckle.

"And you. Your friends are coming over," he reminds me.

"Right."

"You don't want them to?"

"No. Yes. Sam can't come, so it just won't be as fun." I shrug.

"If you're not in the mood for a party, just cancel."

"It's not really a party. We'll probably just eat and watch films with a glass of wine."

"You'll be drinking?" Doc frowns, disapprovingly.

"Yes, Doctor. A glass of wine or two. You are aware that I'm twenty-three, right?"

"I'm aware." He nods.

My heart flutters.

I roll my eyes. Get a grip, Shelby. The man is successful and super-hot.

Dr. Moore's smile drops. "What have I told you about rolling your eyes, young lady?"

I swallow at his sharp tone. It should not have the effect it does. "It's rude," I reply breathily.

His eyes drop to my lips just as the bottom one disappears between my teeth.

Doc frowns. The man probably thinks I'm on the verge of a breakdown . . . and I am. Just not for the reason he thinks.

Needing a minute to myself, I wait at the end of the drive while Riley and Leonard knock on the white door.

By the time they rejoin me, I've talked myself down.

The next few houses are done with Riley between us, her hands clasped in ours.

The street is lively and loud as costumed children run from house to house. A small group of older girls walks toward us, their voices loud. I'd know that god-awful screech anywhere. Kitty Newman. The girl who tortured me through high school. Queen bee, head cheerleader, and sister to Riley's classmate, Max Newman.

She eyes my snowman onesie like she wants to burn it with me still inside. It's worlds apart from her slutty nurse outfit. I try to ignore her, but we're heading straight for each other.

"Nerdy is definitely not the new sexy," she snarks to her friends. To make it obvious who she means, Kitty looks straight at me.

My cheeks flush, but I do what I did all through high school. I stay quiet and keep walking, but my escape comes to an abrupt halt.

"Off to a party, Miss Newman?"

"Hi, Doc. I didn't see you there."

The suggestive tone makes my stomach roil. *Gross.* Needing to look at anything but her pushing her chest toward my neighbor, I reach out for the bag Leonard holds.

The tall man turns to me as I take the bag from his tight grip. Reaching in, I grab a bottle of water and turn my back on the group of girls.

"You should join us, Leo."

She calls him Leo? Disappointment fills me.

"I'm thirty-eight, not twenty-three, Miss Newman. My partying days are over. I'd rather spend time with my family."

My heart soars when I see him motion toward us out of the corner of my eye. Clearly, he means Riley, but the look of shock on Kitty's face is well worth whatever rumor she starts.

"Miss Newman, remember what I said about being safe. We wouldn't want you in my office again, would we?"

I choke at the implication. Water sprays out, back into the bottle and down my chin. Coughing, I bend slightly, trying to catch my breath.

"And it's Dr. Moore," he corrects her earlier words.

I guess she doesn't call him Leo. My lips twitch, but I fight my grin.

Stepping close to Riley and me, he dismisses Kitty.

"Are you okay?"

I nod, unable to answer.

"I don't like her," Riley mutters, watching the blonde stomp away.

"Enough of that," Doc says, then nods at the house that we're standing in front of. "Go get more candy."

Not needing to be told twice, Riley runs off excitedly.

Once she's out of earshot, I apologize. "Sorry about that. She's not really a fan."

"What's not to love?" He winks, reaching for the water in my hand.

"Oh, don't drink that. I . . ."

But he doesn't wait for me to finish. Tilting the bottle, he gulps some of the water down.

"Spat water back in," I finish in a mumble.

He raises a brow, screwing the cap back on the bottle. "I'm not worried about catching something from you."

I flush at his wink.

A yellow blur flies past us, little feet slapping the sidewalk. "To the next!"

Using the distraction, I follow the little girl.

"I missed you in my office this week."

My heart stops at his words. "What do you mean?" We both know what he's referring to. I just never expected him to acknowledge it out loud.

"Your annual visit," he challenges, his left brow raised.

My face flames at his words. I go to see him as a patient after Halloween for one reason only. My mystery man. There's nowhere else in this small town to go for Plan B and a checkup.

A secret that has stayed between Doc; Kathy, his receptionist; and me until now.

I glare at him for saying the words out loud and in public.

"It wasn't needed this year," I snap.

Leonard looks away.

Shit.

An awkward silence settles over the two of us. Riley skips a few feet in front, oblivious to my torn morals.

"I'm sorry. It's just a sore subject."

"I understand." He nods. "I shouldn't have inquired. I'm sorry."

Scrubbing my face, I sigh. "It's just complicated."

"You and your boyfriend have a falling-out?"

"I don't have a boyfriend."

"Your visits suggest otherwise," he argues.

Does fucking someone once a year make him my boyfriend? Can I even call it fucking when I don't remember what we do?

"It's . . ."

"Complicated?" he finishes for me.

"Yeah," I breathe.

"Anything worth having usually is."

I swallow at his deep tone.

"Maybe. Maybe not," I mumble.

I don't get to mull over Doc's words for long.

"Daddy!" Riley yells from farther along the sidewalk, pointing at a house with their porch light on.

"I'm coming. Go knock on it."

The little girl drops her arm. "You're my Pokeball. I can't keep going without you," she tells him, taking his hand as soon as he's close enough. They walk up the path together. "That would be silly."

"Yeah, Daddy. Don't be silly," I taunt.

His only response is a small glare over the top of Riley's head.

CHAPTER THREE

Leonard

My fingers twitch with the need to hold Shelby's hand. My skin tingles with the knowledge of her being within touching distance.

Over a year. That's how long it's been since I had my hands on her. Checking on her at the Cromwell cabin a few days ago doesn't count. I didn't get to caress her, fuck her, fill her. Instead, I'd been on the verge of a heart attack.

It had taken everything in me not to yell at her. Why did she stay with Kaleb? Why didn't she come to me to keep her safe? Why didn't she make herself available to me?

I'd gone to her on Halloween as I have for years, but the house had been empty. The glass of apple juice was still on her bedside table where I'd left it.

Shelby is right about two things. Our relationship is complicated, and tonight is a new Halloween. A redo of the night we missed earlier this week.

My heart stutters when we stop in front of my driveway. Tonight was a success in every way. Riley got a huge haul of candy, and Shelby was more open than ever before. I just need her to see me as more than a doctor and her older neighbor.

Riley opens her candy bag, offering the contents to Shelby. "I picked a Mounds bar out for you." My sweet girl smiles.

"You did?" Shelby asks in surprise, her right hand moving to rest over her heart. "Muffin, you didn't have to do that."

Riley shrugs. "You said they were your favorite."

Shelby stares at my daughter for a second before stepping forward and encasing her sweet face between her hands.

"They are. My dad used to buy me one every Halloween because no one really gives out coconut candy." Shelby blinks quickly. "Thank you, muffin."

My heart lurches at the sadness in her voice.

Together, they root through the colorful candy wrappers until they find the one they want. Holding it up like a trophy, Shelby thanks Riley again with a tight hug.

Releasing my daughter, she turns to envelop me too.

"Thank you for letting me tag along. It was fun, and I really needed this."

Her body pulls away from mine far too quickly, but given the movement in my pants, it's probably for the best.

As I watch her disappear into her home, my cock stays awake. Stirring at what is to come. After tonight, this year will be different. I'm not waiting another year to touch her again.

I want her. In my home, in my bed, in my life.

After tonight, everything changes.

Happy Halloween, baby.

CHAPTER FOUR

Shelby

Pulling the cork from the bottle, I can't fight my smile.

Pouring a little into the glass, I take a small sip.

"Hmm," I hum in approval.

Of course it's good, as if Dr. Moore would gift a wine that was anything but.

Topping up my own glass, I move on to the other four. Leonard's earlier words clatter around my head.

"No more than one glass of wine."

I still feel the heat of his touch on my chin. He'd forced my gaze to his and made me repeat his words. He'd said the wine was a thank you for trick-or-treating, but I think he just didn't want us getting drunk on cheap wine and making a lot of noise.

Not that I would. I'm a good neighbor, or at least I try to be. The thought of Leonard being disappointed or angry with me makes my stomach hurt. So one glass it is.

Carefully, I join my friends in the living room. *Jigsaw* is paused and ready to go on the television.

"Wine?" Edward frowns.

"Yeah." I nod. "There are a few beers in the fridge if you want them?"

"He'll take the wine. Thank you." Emma smiles, taking two glasses from me. Passing one to the man slouched behind her, the blonde elbows her boyfriend.

"Wine's perfect. Thank you, Shelby."

Laughing, I pass Joe and Mark theirs before sitting on the other sofa opposite the armchair Joe and his boyfriend share.

How am I fifth wheeling at my own party?

Kitty.

According to Edward, Kitty went all out in spreading the word of her own get-together, which was being hosted at her boyfriend's house.

But the truth is, I don't mind. The only two people I'd want here who aren't are Sam and my mystery man.

The two couples who did show up were more than happy with food, alcohol, and scary films.

Sipping my wine, I tug down the throw from behind me and tuck my feet under myself.

Fuck Kitty and her slutty outfit. I've had a great night, and it's only going to get better.

Friends and good vibes.

What more could a girl want?

CHAPTER FIVE

Shelby

Fuck, my head hurts.

Opening my eyes, I immediately regret it when pain stabs my forehead.

Squeezing my eyes closed, I curse. "Fuck." My voice is husky and thick.

Déjà vu hits.

I've woken up feeling like this before. The past few Halloweens.

He was here.

My mystery man.

But something is different because between my legs isn't the only thing aching. My throat feels scratchy. Raw. Heat fills my face as I take stock of my body. My back entrance is sore too . . . and wet.

I bite my lip as I roll from my stomach to my

back, frowning when my body protests. My muscles cry out at the move. I don't know whether to laugh or cry.

He was here, and he was angry. He wanted me to know it. Maybe because I wasn't here on Halloween?

Looking around the room, I can see Edward and Emma fast asleep on the other sofa, while Mark and Joe are out like a light on the armchair, curled around each other.

Squinting, I wait for my eyes to adjust to the morning light streaming in through the large windows.

What the hell happened last night?

The last thing I remember was sitting down to watch the film. Everything after that is a haze and then nothing.

Pushing out a loud breath, I turn my head slowly. The DVD box on the floor shows we never got to the second film. I try to remember more, but only snippets of laughing with my friends come to me.

It's no good. I won't remember. The past has taught me that.

Slowly, I push up. My left arm is braced behind me while I drag myself up with my right using the sofa cushion.

Once on my feet, I'm unsteady and slightly nauseous. It'll pass. It always does.

How did he drug me? But as soon as the question enters my mind, I push it out. I've never figured it out before. It's not worth the brain power, especially when I feel like this.

Fuck it. Does it really matter? He'll still do it again next year anyway.

My heart races at the idea, and my inner walls clench.

Shelby, you have issues. I roll my eyes.

Creeping out of the room, I try not to wake the others. I feel shaky, as if my bones are made of jelly, yet I'm also lax and relaxed.

In the bathroom, I lean against the door and blow out another breath. *Come on, Shelby.* I silently urge myself to get it together. This isn't the first time I've woken feeling the effects of whatever he gives me and a pleasurable soreness in my body.

But in a way it is. Last night was the first time he's used anything other than my pussy, and my God, do I feel it.

Licking my dry lips, I push off the door. A disheveled, wide-eyed version of myself stares back from the large mirror above the sink.

My reflection shows confusion. I'd been sure he wouldn't come tonight. After all, it's not Halloween. I guess even he was thrown off by the burglaries. Biting my lip, I blink, watching my cheeks heat, and the color finally returning.

Leaning on the sink, I bend at the hips and take deep cleansing breaths. Something taps against the inside of my top as I shift. Pulling at the neck of my top, I peer inside. A gold locket hangs around my neck.

My brows furrow. I don't wear a necklace.

Holy shit! He gave me a gift.

Warmth spreads through me. *This isn't just fucking for him either.*

I may have woken up sore and confused, but the one thing I'm not is afraid or disappointed. Staying over at Kaleb's, I'd known that he might not come for me, but I'd hoped. But given what Kaleb had done to the two men who broke into his house, it's probably for the best that my mystery man stayed away.

I'm glad he came here instead. Speaking of, I need a shower. My throat screams every time I swallow. My face heats further. How do I explain this to Dr. Moore? *You don't.* The same thing I tell him every time I've been before, I say the bare minimum.

The mission for today is to check that I'm not injured and get birth control.

Splashing my face, I let out a deep sigh. My chest feels light.

He came for me.

A bright smile spreads across my face.

He came for me.

CHAPTER SIX

Leonard

My eyes find the clock sitting on the white wall of my office. 11:03. Concern and irritation battle inside me. Shelby's appointment was at eleven.

The pen in my hand clicks over and over, my thumb relentlessly pressing the top.

Where's my girl?

"Hi, dear. The doctor is ready for you. Go right in," Kathy greets.

Hearing my receptionist, I stand and then sit. *Shit,* what's the matter with me? Last night wasn't our first time, so why do I feel antsy?

Shelby enters my office with a deep blush.

Smiling, I stand and motion to the chair in front of my desk. "Have a seat."

My eyes roam over her, assessing the way she walks. Her gait appears normal, good. I'd been rough last night, but I want her sore, not in pain.

"Shelby." I nod. "What can I do for you? Kathy said you were a little vague when booking the appointment."

"Thanks for making room to see me." Her eyes flit about the room.

"Shelby," I urge.

"So you know how we were talking about my . . . erm, annual checkup. Turns out I do need that."

Nodding, I give her an easy smile, encouraging her to continue. I may know why she's here, but I want to hear it.

I need her to say it.

My office falls into silence as we look at each other. Finally, Shelby rolls her eyes and caves.

"I need an exam and Plan B. Please," she adds politely.

"Don't roll your eyes," I reprimand. "Let's complete your examination first, shall we?"

Swallowing, Shelby heaves a breath before following me to the door connecting to the examination room attached to my office.

She moves shyly at first but raises her chin as she passes me. *That's my girl.* "Go ahead and undress. Everything's set up and ready for you."

Busying myself, I pluck a pair of gloves from the box sitting by the door. "With you wanting Plan B, I assume you had vaginal sex?" I ask. I can't help myself.

Without turning, I know her cute face is bright red. The shuffling of clothes stops, and I hear her climb onto the bench. Steadying my breath, I will my body not to react.

"Yes," she answers reluctantly.

"Anything else I need to know?" I push, taking a seat on my stool. Wheeling closer, I settle between her spread legs, taking my pre-prepped table with me.

"Erm."

I watch her squirm both physically and mentally.

Huffing, Shelby lays her head back and gives in. "We had anal sex last night."

I grin, safely hidden between her legs. "And?" I stress, knowing that there's more to say.

"I performed oral . . . I think."

"You think?"

"It's complicated."

"Shelby, do I need to worry?" I play along, adding lubricant to two fingers.

"No!" she rushes. "He wouldn't hurt me, not like that."

"Good." I squeeze her inner thigh. "This will be a little cold," I warn.

Shelby's body tenses as I ease my fingers into her. A whimper of pain drifts down the table.

"Relax, it's just me," I reassure.

Four words I shouldn't have said. My body reacts instantly. Memories flood me of being braced above her, easing my cock into her sleepy body. I half expect her to whisper, "Hi," back. But this isn't Halloween, we're not in her bedroom, and she's not on the brink of a drug-induced sleep.

The memory of our previous Halloween floods me—the way she smiled to greet me, the way she looked when she realized who I was, the way she whispered, "Hi," shyly when I joined her on the bed. Her pleas and moans sound out in my head, something that's getting harder and harder to wait a full year to hear again.

Pushing down on her lower belly with my right hand, I try to stay focused on her exam.

We both ignore the way that her body responds, or at least pretend we do. Shelby squeezes her eyes closed while I pretend that I can't feel the heat and added lubricant her body is providing.

My girl wants me. She just won't acknowledge it, at least not in the light of day.

"Seems to be the usual. Your lovemaking was rough, but he was careful," I reassure, removing my wet fingers.

"Lovemaking?" she asks, confused.

I see her frown as I stand.

"Lovemaking." I nod. "You're a little puffy. Are you in pain?" I ask, touching a finger to her glistening lower lips.

I didn't think her face could heat further, but I was wrong.

She answers silently with a shake of her head.

"Out loud."

"I'm okay."

I raise a brow. I'd been angry about missing out on spending Halloween with her, so I'd fucked her hard.

"A little sore."

Better.

"Take a few hot baths. Soaking in warm water will help soothe it."

Shelby nods again. "Okay," she rushes to add.

Good girl.

"I'm just going to check back here." I prepare her, regloving and recoating my fingers. "Was last night your first time having anal sex?"

"Yes," she pants, biting her lip.

"Were there any issues?"

"No, everything was good. Just sore this morning."

I know she's lying. There's no way that she remembers, but my heart warms at the strength in her answer. She trusts that it was good, that her mystery man took care of her, and I did.

My lips twitch at the name. It's what she calls me, right before recognition settles across her face, quickly followed by lust, always.

And it was good. Phenomenal, actually. The fact that her friends had been passed out in the same room had only heightened the experience . . . for both of us.

"You're perfect," I tell her honestly, withdrawing from her body.

Removing my gloves, I step back as Shelby pulls her legs from the stirrups and sits up. Before she can jump down, I step forward again.

"Let's have a look at that throat," I insist.

Holding her chin with one hand, I reach for a tongue depressor.

Tilting her head, I peer inside. "The back of your throat is irritated also, but it's nothing that lozenges and a few warm drinks won't cure." Releasing her chin, I stay close, with her trapped on the exam table.

Shelby has folded her hands to rest them at the apex of her thighs, but it's not enough to shield her naked bottom half.

I frown, not enjoying her shyness as much as usual. I want her to be comfortable around me. *I want her to know who I am.* Surprised at the force of the thought, I step back. Once a year isn't enough, and the knowledge that I have to wait makes me grumpy.

"Dress and join me in my office," I offer sullenly.

Sitting at my desk, I pinch the bridge of my nose.

"Everything okay?" Shelby asks, standing in the doorway.

"Of course." I smile, waving to the chair she occupied earlier. "In regard to a prescription, I'm not giving any. You have some discomfort to be expected from rough intercourse, but I believe that was the point." I smirk. "Instead, I recommend rest and warm baths. You should be back to normal within a day or so."

"And the Plan B?" she asks after a few seconds.

I make a disgruntled sound and reach for my prescription pad. "We've discussed this a few times, and I thought I was clear last year. He has a say in whether you have a child or not. It's a decision to be made together. An old-fashioned view, maybe," I acknowledge, "but it's my opinion that matters here. Did you discuss what you'd like to do about birth control with your boyfriend?"

"I told you it's complicated. I don't have a boyfriend, and it's my choice."

"Well, I'll uncomplicate it. This is the last time that I prescribe Plan B, and I'm not putting you on birth control until the two of you have a conversation about what you both want and come to an agreement." I hold out the piece of paper after tearing it off the pad, knowing that when that conversation happens, my girl will know exactly who's been breaking into her house. "And I'll know if you're lying, Shelby."

Her brow furrows as she accepts the prescription. "Thank you." Shelby hesitates before adding, "We talked about condoms . . . kind of. He wasn't really a fan."

I chuckle at the memory.

Brushing the bangs off her forehead, I greet her sleepy gaze with a smile.
"I'm late. You should be asleep by now."

Shelby shakes her head clumsily. "Nope. I knew you would come."

"Of course. I would have been here sooner, but Riley refused to settle down. Too much candy." I roll my eyes before turning them to the clock on her bedside. 11:58. I tut when I see what sits beside the digital clock.

"Use a condom?" she whispers, biting her lip, her voice so timid that the order sounds like a plea.

"No," I answer with a shake of my head and a firm tone. I give her a small smile to take away the sting of my rebuttal. Rubbing my nose against hers, I breathe her in before pressing a small kiss to her now parted lips.

"Happy Halloween, sweetheart."

Of course, the only memory Shelby will have from that conversation is the consequences. A sliced condom on the table top. A clear message. I'm not interested in using them.

And birth control is out of the question while she remains oblivious to who I am. It'd be giving her a green light to find someone else. *Fuck no!*

"Well, not everyone likes using them," I offer unhelpfully.

Folding my hands on my desk, I give a look that says our conversation is over, because it is.

"Okay." Shelby squirms. "Well, thank you for this." She waves the prescription.

"Make sure to rest and take baths."

My stomach twists as she turns to leave.

As I watch her walking out the door, a thought occurs to me not for the first time. *Who says I have to wait a year?*

CHAPTER SEVEN

Shelby

Well, that could have gone worse . . . not!

Shoving another forkful of frosting-covered cake into my mouth, I groan.

I nearly orgasmed on my doctor's fingers. My doctor, who also happens to be my hot neighbor. At least one of us stayed professional.

Or not, I smirk.

I hadn't been the only one affected. Doc just hid it better, but nothing was hiding THAT bulge. Some of my self-loathing and embarrassment melts away.

Get a grip. I mentally slap myself. What would a gorgeous thirty-eight-year-old doctor want with a part-time barista?

Rolling my eyes, I stab a larger piece of cake with my fork and stuff it in my mouth. Besides, how would

I explain my yearly visitor? Would my mystery man be jealous?

Raising a brow, I contemplate the thought, but before I can get dragged into what-ifs, a timid knock sounds at my front door. It was so quiet that if I'd had the TV on, I wouldn't have heard it.

Pushing away from the kitchen island, I place my fork next to the tray of half-eaten birthday cake.

A second knock sounds as I'm crossing the living room, this one a little more insistent.

Turning the lock, I grip the handle and open my mouth to greet whoever it is on the other side, but the words die before they can escape.

Instead, I stand wide-eyed and open-mouthed, staring at a crying Riley.

"Muffin." I finally manage to squeeze out.

The little girl rushes forward, wrapping her arms around my waist, her sobs muffled by my sweater.

"Baby, what happened?" I ask, folding myself and pulling her closer.

Her crying continues as I stroke her hair back. My mind races with all kinds of scenarios, but she's here, with no broken bones and no blood. That's what matters.

I kiss the top of her brown curls and remind her over and over that everything's going to be okay, until she calms enough that I can pull away.

Kneeling, I wipe her cheeks dry and brush away the brown strands stuck to her face. "Are you hurt?"

Sniffling, Riley shakes her head.

"What happened?" I whisper.

"Miss Sarah was watching me, but then a boy came, and she left."

My heart beats for the first time since I opened the door, breaking free of the fear that froze it.

"Sarah left?" I repeat.

Riley nods, wiping under her nose with the back of her hand.

"When did she leave, muffin?"

The little girl shrugs. "I waited, but she never came back, and I got scared. Daddy says I'm not allowed outside without telling anyone, but I didn't have anyone to tell."

"Well, you did super good coming here, and I'll make sure your daddy knows how good you did," I praise, pressing a kiss to her forehead. "Are you hungry?"

Riley nods quickly, and her tummy lets out a well-timed growl.

Pulling a shocked face, I temper down the fury roaring through me. What kind of moron leaves a six-year-old home alone?

A dead one!

No, no. We can't go around killing irresponsible teenage sitters, *can we?*

Standing, I hold out my hand for her to take. "How about we go lock up your house, and I'll call your dad to let him know that you're safe?"

Riley nods, letting me lead her out. Closing my front door, I lock it. I might only be popping into my neighbor's house, but after four years of my mystery visitor, I never leave it open. Ever.

Unlike Doc's house.

The front door opens with a flick of my wrist. I keep Riley close and do a quick walk-through just to confirm no one is inside and then head for the fridge. That's where every parent leaves the emergency contacts, right?

Smiling at my own genius, I pluck the sticky note off the fridge door.

"Bingo. Do you know where the front door key is, muffin?"

She points at a bowl near the entrance.

"Perfect. Do you wanna grab some toys or coloring stuff to bring with you?" I check.

Riley nods and lets go of my hand.

I watch her run down the hall and into her bedroom before I reach for my cell in my back pocket. The line rings four times before the practice's receptionist, Kathy, picks up.

"Dr. Moore's office, how can I help?"

"Hi, this is Shelby. Can I speak to Dr. Moore, please?"

"He's with a patient."

I frown at her sharp tone.

"Can you ask him to call me back when he's free, please?"

"This isn't a social club. This is a doctor's office. If you need to see the doctor, you need to make an appointment like everyone else."

I blink at her harsh response. What crawled up her ass? *Fine.*

"And what time is available today?"

"Other than the last slot of the day at five, he's all booked up."

"Sounds perfect. Five it is." I smirk.

"And what should I put as your issue?"

"A pain in the ass," I mutter dryly.

All sound from the other end of the line ceases, before a clipped, "We'll see you at five," sounds.

What is wrong with people today?

I'm sure any mention of Riley would have gotten me through to Leonard, but I feel like being petty. Besides, he'd only worry about Riley for the rest of the day. We'll have a little girls' day and go surprise him with an early finish by being his last appointment.

Speaking of, I watch as Riley drags a heavy-looking backpack down the carpeted hall.

"Muffin, what did you pack?" I laugh.

A cheeky grin is her only answer.

CHAPTER EIGHT

Leonard

Grumbling, I move the mouse on my desktop and click on my calendar. Kathy added an appointment to the end of the day, something she knows I hate, but when someone needs me, they need me.

Hopefully, it's something simple, and I can be home in the next thirty minutes. I've been anxious since leaving Riley with Sarah this morning. I glance at my phone lying next to my computer, but there's still no update on my daughter and her day so far.

The girl is not my favorite babysitter, but with my regular nanny moving away to be closer to her grandchildren, I didn't have many options. Besides, I've used Sarah before, and it worked out fine. Did she clean up after their messy play? No. Did she give me updates throughout the day? Also no. But beggars can't be choosers, and everyone can't be Mrs. Mears.

Hopefully, she and her son drive each other mad, and the older lady rushes back to town by New Year's.

I chuckle at the thought and turn back to work.

"Shelby," I whisper, confused. Why is my woman making another appointment? Not that I mind seeing her twice in one day. Clicking on the notes, I read the comment. *Pain in the rear.*

Fuck! I hurt her! *Fuck, fuck, fuck!*

I should have been gentler for her first time. I didn't stretch her out. I'd wanted her to feel it in the moment, but I didn't want her injured. She'd seemed fine earlier.

The door to my office starts to open, and I stand to greet her, to reassure her that whatever the issue is, I'll sort it. But the words die when a giggle floats in.

I know that cute sound anywhere.

"Hi, baby." I grin before I even see her.

Riley pushes in, stumbling when the door moves quicker than she does.

"Careful, muffin."

My gaze snaps back to the doorway where Shelby steps in with a timid "forgive me" smile.

Stepping out from behind my desk, I crouch, enveloping my sweet girl into a bear hug. Squeezing tight, I rock us side to side.

Framing her face, I ask, "You hungry?" I don't ask why she's with the woman I'm obsessed with because whatever the reason, I already know I'm about to be furious, and that's not my baby's fault.

She's with Shelby, so I know she's safe and unharmed, and that's the most important thing. I'll deal with Sarah later.

"Uh-huh." She nods.

"How do you ladies feel about Soul of Italy for dinner tonight?"

"Yes!" Riley yells, jumping up and down, waving the doll in her hand.

Shelby pauses. Before she can decline the offer, I push forward.

"It's the least I can do," I insist, gesturing to Riley.

Standing, I use my full height to crowd Shelby. At six foot, the height difference is just enough that she needs to strain her neck back.

"Carbs sound good," she breathes.

Good. I don't want to have to strong-arm her in front of Riley, especially if I'm about to get mad.

Stepping away, I retreat just long enough to grab my suit jacket, briefcase, and cell phone.

"Ladies first." I gesture with my left hand.

Switching my briefcase to the other hand, I place my right palm on Shelby's lower back. Together, we pause for Riley to skip ahead, then follow.

"Kathy, I'm finished for the day. Please close everything down. I'll be back in a minute to lock up, and then you can go on and head home."

My receptionist frowns. "Wasting an appointment that someone else needed is impolite."

I feel Shelby's back straighten beneath my hand. "Did someone else call needing to see the doctor?"

"No."

"Then it wasn't wasted."

I look back and forth between the two normally polite women, clearly missing something. But it doesn't matter, nor does it matter that Kathy has worked for me since we moved to town. I'll always side with Shelby.

"You can call and make an appointment anytime," I approve, rubbing my thumb back and forth.

She shivers under my touch.

Shelby opens her mouth to explain, but I shake my head. "Not here."

I walk my girls to my car parked out front. Opening the back door, I turn my attention to Shelby as Riley climbs into the back seat. "Wait for me."

Buckling my little girl in safely, I close the back to find Shelby closing the front passenger door behind herself.

Tutting, I pull the door handle. Grasping the seat belt, I lean over Shellby to buckle her into place. Happy she's secure, I drop to a crouch in the open doorway. "What was I unclear about?"

Shelby's cheeks flush.

"When I say wait, I mean wait." I pause, watching her features shroud in confusion. "You don't open a door when I'm here to do it for you. It's bad manners on my part."

Shelby frowns. "I can open a door."

"I know." I nod. "But I'd rather do it."

She stares at me for a moment before nodding. "Okay."

"Okay?" I check.

"Okay," she agrees with an easy shrug.

Happy that she's not fighting me on this, I knock her under the chin with my forefinger as I stand. "Good girl."

Carefully, I close the door, then head to the office to lock up just as Kathy leaves the building.

CHAPTER NINE

Shelby

Blowing out a breath, I try to cool my face. Why is Leonard insisting I follow an order so hot? *Get a grip, Shelby.*

But instead of arguing that it's not 1912 and I can open any damn door I want, I'm sitting here with a flushed face and wet panties.

Is that what it's like with my mystery man? Does he take charge? Do I even wake up for him? But the truth is, the answers don't matter because when I wake up, the feelings left in my body are arousal and contentment. Whatever happens in the time I lose each year is something that I very much want and crave.

Is that why I feel like I'm cheating?

Going out for dinner with Doc and Riley is the

closest thing to a date that I've ever had. How can I date when I already have a man that I want, even if I don't know who he is? But as Leo slides into the seat beside me, it doesn't feel wrong. In fact, nothing has felt this right in a long time.

Lost in thought, I startle when a large hand squeezes my knee.

"Sorry, I didn't mean to scare you."

"No, I'm sorry. I was a million miles away."

I expect him to pull away, but the longer his hand stays there, the damper my panties get.

"Why is Riley with you?"

I roll my eyes, earning a squeeze from his hand. A warning.

"Sorry," I mutter, remembering his past reprimands. This man is all about manners. Disappointment fills me when his hand joins the other on the steering wheel. "Riley came over to my house a few hours ago. She was crying and scared."

Doc looks at me for a second before turning back to the road. "Where was Sarah?" he asks, his tone brimming with disbelief.

"I don't know." I shrug. "Riley said someone came to the house, and she left."

"She left my six-year-old home alone?"

His knuckles whiten as he tightens his grip on the wheel.

"She's okay," I whisper.

I don't know what comes over me as I reach out and squeeze his thigh. I've lost my damn mind. I feel his body tense under his suit pants and quickly pull my hand away. At least Cromwell is a small town. It won't take long to walk home when he kicks me out of his car.

But Dr. Moore doesn't slam on the brakes and shove me out of the car. Instead, his hand finds mine. His long fingers wrap around my hand before dragging them back to his lap. The back of my hand rests against his thigh, and his thumb rubs back and forth as if to soothe me, but one look at his face makes it clear that he's the one who needs calming.

Wiggling my fingers, I squirm in his grasp until he releases my hand enough that I can entwine my fingers with his. Pulling his hand over, I set it in my lap and encase his hand in both of mine.

"Riley is perfect."

Leo nods.

"Say it."

"Riley is okay." He nods, his eyes flicking to his daughter through the rearview mirror.

"She said perfect, Daddy," the little girl in the back corrects while looking out the window.

Leo's whole body relaxes, all tension puffing out with his laugh. Pulling into the restaurant parking lot, Leonard looks back through the mirror.

"Riley is sassy."

"Perfect." She laughs, grinning at her dad.

Parking, he counters, "Riley is silly."

"Perfect." She shakes her head.

Turning off the ignition, Doc turns in his seat, facing her. "Riley is beautiful."

"Dadddyyy," she whines around a giggle.

"Riley is perfect," he whispers. "Were you hurt while waiting for Miss Sarah?"

"No," Riley whispers back, all traces of humor gone. "I was just scared, but then I thought of Shelby, so I went to her."

"You did the right thing." He smiles. "Don't forget Princess Penny," he reminds her, nodding to her doll lying on the back seat beside her.

"Wait for me," he orders, finally letting go of my hand.

I miss him instantly.

Get a grip. I roll my eyes at myself.

The door beside me opens a few seconds later. Surprised and still a little in shock at my earlier bold actions, I remain seated as he reaches across me to release the seat belt. Curling my lips inward, I try not to react as his chest brushes mine, but there's no hiding my flushed face.

God, I'm pathetic.

Taking his offered hand, I climb out, holding my breath when the front of my body touches his again when Leo fails to step back.

Closing the car door, he stares down at me with a heated gaze.

Swallowing, I bat away the fantasies that swarm me. How can I be this hot and bothered over nothing? Doc steps closer, and I step back until I have nowhere to go. With my back against the side of the car, I quickly find myself boxed in. Strong hands settle on the roof of his car on either side of me.

Would it be cheating if I kissed him? Of course not, I don't even know who my mystery man is. So then why do I feel so crummy?

Why did I have to have a neighbor who looks this good?

"Roll your eyes again. I dare you."

I gulp at his words, and a pulse beats heavy between my legs. I don't think once a year is working for me.

Doc's deep rumble brings me out of my thoughts. "Thank you for taking care of her."

My gaze drops to his mouth. "I tried to call, but Kathy wouldn't put me through. Said I couldn't see you without an appointment, hence . . ." I shrug.

Leo frowns. "Kathy knows to always put you through. Perhaps I wasn't clear enough. I'll rectify it tomorrow."

Confusion fills me at his words. Did he know something like this would happen?

"I'll give you my cell number before you go home."

Unable to say anything, I just nod. I watch as his lips spread into a smirk. Blinking, I raise my eyes to his and flush. He caught me staring.

"Thank you," he says again.

Needing to defuse the tension, I shrug nonchalantly. "Don't thank me yet. I may or may not have fed her cake for lunch."

Leo raises a brow. Pushing off the car, he moves to the back door. "May or may not have? Something tells me you did."

"She was crying, and I was eating cake when she knocked."

Like the good dad he is, Leo gives me a disapproving look.

Drawing in a deep breath, I breathe for what feels like the first time since he climbed into the car.

"You had cake for lunch?" he asks his daughter, opening the door for her.

Climbing out of the car, Riley turns to me and then back to her father. A cheeky smile is the only answer he gets.

CHAPTER TEN

Shelby

"Can we have dessert after?" Riley pleads, skipping beside her dad as we follow the hostess.

Doc makes a disgruntled sound. "Depends. How much cake did you have earlier?" he asks, turning to me.

Holding my thumb and forefinger about an inch apart, I answer, "Only a little."

Stopping beside the table, Riley faces us, and holding up her hand, she copies my action.

"Really?" her dad asks, his tone skeptical.

Silent, he arches a brow, looking first at me and then at his daughter. Slowly, Riley's thumb and finger move farther and farther apart.

Laughing, I cover her hand with mine. "Okay,

okay. We ate like a quarter of my birthday cake," I confess.

Placing my hand on top of her head, I spin Riley to face the table and pick her up under her arms. "We're going to have to work on you resisting interrogation," I mutter, sitting her on the chair her dad has pulled out.

"Baby, why don't we lie?" Doc asks Riley, tucking her chair in closer to the table.

"Because it's rude," she answers, swinging her legs.

"So next time I feed her cake for dinner, I should keep it to myself?" I sass.

My body heats when his palm finds the curve of my back.

"Lying by omission is still a lie."

I frown at his pained tone.

"Who are you lying to?" I whisper as I take my seat.

Leo blinks down at me. "Someone who means the world to me, but sometimes it's better than the truth."

I gasp when he places a light kiss on my forehead. Doc freezes for a second before straightening, as if he had done it without thinking. Rounding the table, he kisses the top of Riley's head and takes his own seat.

Seeing the server approach, Leo clears his throat. "What would you ladies like?"

"Spaghetti meatballs, please," Riley rushes.

Biting my lip, I try not to smile at the way she says spaghetti. Why is this girl so fucking cute?

"Me too, please."

"Make that three. Thank you," he orders, closing his menu and handing it to the server. "Would you like wine?" He turns to me.

"No, thank you."

"Three waters, please."

"Great. I'll be right back with your drinks."

"When Riley was younger, she struggled to say spaghetti. After a while, 'speti' kind of stuck," Leonard explains.

The loving look he gives his daughter melts my heart.

"She's perfect," I say, repeating my words from earlier.

"She is," he agrees. Our gaze meets while the warmth of his hand settles on top of mine. I curse my heated cheeks and turn toward Riley, but not before catching sight of Doc's smirk.

Maybe this isn't one-sided after all.

CHAPTER ELEVEN

Leonard

The sound of giggling warms my heart. My cheeks ache from smiling so much throughout dinner.

This time of day is special to me. It doesn't matter how busy I am or who needs me, I always make it home in time for dinner. I worried that Shelby being here would throw off our sense of calm, but if anything, she added to it.

Riley isn't the only one who's perfect.

My baby adores Shelby, a fact I couldn't be happier about. The past two hours have been filled with laughter and love, offering a glimpse into how our future could be.

Will be.

Shelby was made for us, made for me.

"You're great with her," I praise the woman in question.

Shelby blushes. It always gives her away. *I fucking love it.*

"She's not exactly a difficult child."

We walk peacefully toward the parked car, both watching Riley, who remains a few steps ahead.

I see Shelby peek at me a few times, but she remains quiet. I want her to open up to me in her own time. It's what I've always wanted. I just never expected our situation to last this long.

"Don't laugh," she warns, pointing a finger.

I wrap my hand around the offending digit. "Never," I promise.

"Being a mom is all I've ever wanted." She shrugs, as if to make her words seem less than they are. "It's something Lulu and I had in common," she confesses, referring to her childhood friend who moved away last year. "I guess it's why I never went off to college. My dad had a bit to do with that. After he got ill, I didn't even think of leaving. But I never made plans after graduation because all I wanted to do was get married and have babies."

"You never found the right guy?" I whisper, the words choking me. The thought of her wanting those things with another man kills me, and the idea of her doing it . . . over my dead body, or better yet, over his.

Unaware of my sudden need to murder an imaginary man, Shelby shrugs. "Thought I did. But I guess he had other plans."

Good. My heart starts again at the knowledge that no one is vying for her attention.

"Your mystery man." I nod.

My grin gets wider when she reaches up and fiddles with the necklace under her shirt.

My mother's necklace, the one I took off my first wife's body. She didn't deserve it. Ashley lost the right to wear it the minute she betrayed our wedding vows.

"I'm sure the right man knows exactly where to find you."

"Well, he'd better hurry up, because if I spend any more time with Riley, I'm going to get baby fever." She laughs lightly.

"That might be remedied if you both continue not using protection," I warn.

Her cheeks heat. "I told you . . ."

"It's complicated," I finish for her. "It will be when you get pregnant."

And that's exactly what she's going to be. Regret fills me for all the times I wrote her a prescription for Plan B. But she wasn't ready then. And neither was I.

I'm lucky we live in Cromwell. It's a small town. The pharmacy attached to my clinic is the only place to get meds, including some over-the-counter items, unless you're willing to travel. The only way anyone is getting that shit is through me.

My pharmacy, my rules.

One I implemented the day after I took Shelby's virginity.

"Well, look who found himself another victim," a male voice sneers.

And just like that, my good mood is gone.

"Take Riley and get in the car," I order, handing the keys to Shelby. I don't take my eyes off the man approaching.

Kyle Cooper.

"Officer Cooper. I apologize, you lost that job a few years ago. I keep forgetting. Mr. Cooper, is there a reason you're bothering me and my family?"

"Family?" He snorts. "Do you know what kind of man you're fucking?" he shouts, his words aimed at the quickly retreating back of Shelby.

"Lower your fucking voice," I growl.

"What? You don't want the new piece of ass to know about the old one? Or do you just not want her to know what you did?"

My blood heats, racing through my veins with pure hatred. Clearly, losing his job four years ago hadn't been enough. I'd hoped that those Cromwell brothers would have taken care of Cooper by now. If it wasn't so inconvenient, I'd do it myself.

There's still time.

"First of all, I have never had a piece of ass. I had a wife who ran off with her lover, which resulted in my divorcing her. The fact no one can find her is no longer my problem. And second, you ever say anything so vulgar in front of my daughter again, I'll show you exactly the kind of man I am."

My lip curls. He disgusts me.

Picking a fight with me is one thing. After all, the man is right. I did kill her. However, trying to upset Shelby and Riley is another matter.

"You don't scare me." Cooper huffs.

I take a step forward at his words. "Then why are you shaking?" I chuckle, tilting my head. Looking at him from head to toe, I let my true self show.

Stepping back, I keep my eyes on him. Having Shelby again might not be the only thing that can't wait. Cooper might have to be dealt with too.

Once there's sufficient distance between us, I turn sharply and approach the car with hurried steps.

Shelby and Riley are both in the car, and I feel a little calmer.

They're safe.

Joining them, I lock the doors before starting the car.

"I'm sorry about that," I say, looking first at Shelby and then back at Riley.

My little girl looks up from her dolly, Penny, completely oblivious.

Pulling out of the parking lot, I apologize to Shelby again.

"I'm sorry. It won't happen again."

The petite brunette beside me waves off my words. "Don't worry about it. He's mad. Like, you should book him for a seventy-two-hour hold kind of mad. He's been making weird accusations against

Kaleb and his brothers for years. As if there could be three serial killers in Cromwell Town and no one would know." She laughs, rolling her eyes.

I let the action slide because she's right. That is absurd . . . there's four.

Matching her smile, I nod.

"He thinks I . . ." My eyes flit to the rear-view mirror to check Riley is preoccupied before mouthing, "Killed," then say, "my ex-wife."

Shelby rears back as if I slapped her.

"He's obsessed with catching a killer."

"Seems he's in the wrong town because he won't find one here."

My cock stirs when her hand lands on my thigh.

"Are you okay?"

Squeezing her hand, I look from the road to her and back. "I'm perfect."

"That you are," she mutters.

The rest of the drive is done in silence. Shelby doesn't speak up when I take the long way around, adding an extra five minutes onto our journey home. Maybe she thinks I'm worried about Cooper, but the truth is, I'm just not ready to say good night.

Pulling into my drive, I'm filled with disappointment.

"Thank you for dinner," Shelby whispers, climbing from the car.

"It's the least I could do. Thank you for taking care of her."

"Anytime," she offers. "Good night, muffin." She waves to Riley through the window.

I frown, watching her walk away. After tonight, nothing will ever be the same. Shelby is mine and has been since I crawled into her bed four years ago.

It's about time she and everyone else knew it.

CHAPTER TWELVE

Shelby

Curling my hand into a fist, I starfish my body and stretch. Then I roll onto my back and let out a loud groan.

My muscles pull tight before my limbs drop back to the mattress. I feel achy and sated.

My eyes pop open.

Achy, sated, and sore.

Shoving my hand beneath the sheet, I dip my fingers under the band of my pajamas and between my legs.

Wetness greets me.

He was here!

Pulling my hand out, I curse. "Shit!" We didn't use a condom. No way Doc will give me Plan B again.

Groaning, I roll my eyes. I didn't think I needed to have them yet, not until next Halloween.

I took Plan B yesterday, so it'll be okay, right?

Craning my neck, I peer over at the bedside clock. 9:30. How long ago did he leave?

Sitting up quickly, I snatch my cell off the table and scrabble across the bed. Darting from room to room, I search for him, but no one's here. I knew he wouldn't be, but a girl can hope.

I can feel the ache of him deep inside as I walk to the front door on steady feet, no dizziness in sight.

Locked, just like I left it.

How the fuck does he get in? I shrug the thought off quickly, because the truth is, I don't care.

He came for me, again.

Is this the end of our yearly visits? Will he come again tonight? God, I hope so.

My pulse pounds, and my inner muscles squeeze in anticipation, making me hiss. I've been sore before, but not like this.

I know what we do is rough, or at least I think so. Once a year, I wake up bone tired with an equal amount of contentment.

But with no time between his visits, my body isn't used to it. I've never felt better.

Turning the lock, I yank the front door open. Messy hair and in pajamas, I look like a crazy lady. I know I do, but that doesn't stop me from stepping out.

Left and right, I look up and down the quiet

street, but no one is in sight. My shoulders drop. I know I shouldn't be disappointed, but I am.

Who is he?

Suddenly very aware of the wetness between my legs, I squirm. I have a man's semen leaking out of me, and I don't even know his name. Shame burns my face.

Maybe I should text Sam. My best friend won't judge me, right?

Remembering the call she had with Kaleb, I form a plan.

Wiping my thumb across the screen of my cell, I send her a text.

You, me, and a bottle of wine, mine tonight.

Her reply comes before I can take more than three steps back toward the house.

Make it two.

Smiling, I agree.

It's a date!

Although it's probably not the best idea I've ever had. After a full bottle of wine, it won't take much for me to confess my biggest secret to my best friend.

A part of me begs to tell her, but "oh, by the way, a random man has been sneaking into my house and fucking me on Halloween for the past four years" isn't really the type of thing to drop into a conversation.

Plus, what if he stops? Would he call it off if everyone knew? Is he married?

My smile starts to slip, my stomach twisting.

Why can't I know who he is?

"Shelby!"

I spin, tripping over the step. Staggering, I reach out to steady myself on the wall.

Large, warm hands envelop my waist.

Straightening, I come face-to-face with my neighbor.

"Thanks," I breathe.

"What had you so preoccupied?" Leo asks.

Rolling my eyes, I lift the hand holding my cell. "Just making a date."

Something dark flashes over his face.

"With Sam," I rush to add.

"Oh good." He nods.

Our awkward silence is interrupted when a small body wedges between ours. Wrapping her little arms around my legs, Riley grins up at me. "Hi, Shelby."

"Hi, muffin." I chuckle.

Scrunching my face, I check the time. "Shouldn't you be in school?"

"We're running late," Doc says sheepishly.

"Daddy was late," Riley snitches.

"I had a late night." Her dad shrugs.

"We'd best get going. Is Samantha staying the night?"

Wiggling Riley's braid, I smirk. "With how much I plan on drinking, probably."

Doc tilts his head, his look disapproving. "Drink water before bed, not apple juice."

Something in his tone makes me nod.

"I mean it," he doubles down.

"Okay," I whisper. I shouldn't like him being so bossy.

I can't believe he remembers that I drink juice before bed.

"Daddy, I'm telling Miss Lucy that it's your fault we're late."

Leo rolls his eyes. "I'll tell her you had a doctor's appointment."

I laugh, slapping a hand over my mouth.

When he raises a brow, I quip, "Don't roll your eyes, it's rude."

Leonard narrows his eyes and points a finger at me. "Drink water." We watch Riley open the car door and climb in. "No one likes a tattletale," he grumbles lowly before following his daughter.

CHAPTER THIRTEEN

Leonard

Lying in the crawl space of Shelby's attic, I strain to hear any noise from the women below.

Silence greets me.

It's 4 a.m. and my girl and her bestie have been drinking for hours. Apparently, a girls' night is exactly what they needed because after the crying came the laughing.

I hadn't been the only one off my game this morning. Shelby had been distracted and off-kilter when we saw her out front this morning.

Maybe two nights in a row was too much.

It doesn't matter. She'll get used to it.

Used to me.

She'll have to because even the thought of going back to "Halloween only" makes my heart squeeze.

No, Shelby needs to know that I'm not going anywhere. Once she accepts that, I'll tell her who I am. And then we'll be a family.

This had been my fourth Halloween in Cromwell. We moved here for a fresh start, only to find out that my wife's lover had followed us here. Over my dead body or, more accurately, theirs.

The first Halloween had only been a few months after my wife "ran away." Cromwell is a small town. They would not have appreciated me moving on so quickly, especially with a newly turned nineteen-year-old.

But Shelby is twenty-three, and I'm now a divorced single dad. My daughter needs a mother, and I deserve to move on.

Shelby is mine. Always has been.

Forgoing releasing the ladder steps, I grip the edge and lean down until I'm poking out of the loft entrance. Folding, my body curls over until I hang down. Letting go, I drop the few feet into the hallway.

The house is still. Stepping into the living room, I can't stop the grin that spreads across my face.

This woman.

Shelby is draped over one sofa while Samantha is curled up on the other.

Making my way over to her friend, I eye the four bottles of wine on the coffee table. Three empty and one still sealed. Two long-stemmed glasses sit abandoned next to them.

But that's not what has me worried. A pint glass

sits on the side table beside Shelby, and apple juice fills it halfway.

"Shit," I curse.

Grabbing the wool throw, I fan it over Samantha, dipping my hand between her face and the back of the couch cushion.

Hot breath fans my skin.

Huffing out a breath, I turn to the woman responsible for my pounding heart.

As I approach, her eyes flutter drowsily. She's unfocused and dopey.

The way she lies looks awkward and uncomfortable. Her tight jeans don't help, not that she'll have them on for much longer.

Glancing over my shoulder, I check on her friend. Jeans too. *She'll be fine.* Besides, I don't want my girl to get the wrong idea by seeing her friend undressed.

I only have eyes for Shelby.

Crouching, I brush the hair from her eyes. Gray-blue eyes blink back at me. Not quite gray, not quite blue. If anyone were to ask her, she'd say they were blue, but I've stared at them enough to know better.

Blue doesn't do them justice. Her eyes are like the rest of her . . . complicated.

Just like us.

"Did you drink water? Naughty girl."

My question gains me a cute smirk.

"Shelby?" I rouse her with my sharp tone.

"Yep."

"Good."

"See, I'm not naughty."

"This makes you naughty. How much did you drink?" I ask, plucking the pint glass off the side table.

She holds her thumb and forefinger up with a small distance between them. About half the glass.

"And two glasses of wine."

Good. Given what's left in the glass, I believe her. My heart rate slows, returning to a regular pace.

Just enough that she won't remember this in the morning, but not enough to pump her stomach. I place the drink back down. A special concoction made just for my girl.

"I wanted more, but you wouldn't like it."

I rub my thumb below her eye.

"Did Samantha drink any?"

"Nope. Two bottles of wine."

I grin when she holds up three fingers. Wrapping my hand around the digits, I give them a gentle squeeze.

Confused, she tries to sit up. "How did you get in?"

Instead of answering, I chuckle.

"Come," I tell her, gripping her underarms. "Time for bed."

"Okay," Shelby agrees, standing, her earlier words forgotten.

"How was your girls' night?"

"Weird," she whispers, her eyes widening, "Sam and Kaleb, hmm hmm." She clears her throat.

"They what?"

"You know." She waves her hand.

"I don't." I frown.

"Had . . . sex," she whispers so low I barely hear her.

My head rears back. "Really?" I say far too loudly.

"That's what I said!" she rushes. "But don't tell anyone. It's a secret. Shhhh," she pleads, a finger over her mouth.

My chest warms. She trusts me with her friend's secrets.

"I won't tell," I promise.

Leading her into her bedroom, I release her waist just long enough to click the door closed.

Turning, I find Shelby facing me, her plump lip caught between her teeth.

"I have a secret too, but I didn't get to tell her."

I raise a brow. "Oh yeah? What's that, baby?"

"Shhh," she shushes, a finger covering her mouth again.

"Arms up, cutie."

Shelby does as told. Stripping her sweater off, I throw it into the hamper. Her clumsiness from the wine should start to wear off soon. Two glasses don't make her so inebriated that she can't function. And my special mix is for memory and drowsiness.

I want her with me here and now. I just don't want her to remember tomorrow.

"I don't think I have a boyfriend."

My hands still on the button of her pants.

"No?"

"No." She shakes her head. "A lover, a friend with benefits, a fuck buddy." Shelby gives a sharp nod. "A fuck buddy," she decides.

"That's not what we are, Shelby." I tell her, my tone sharp.

Her body rocks as I snap her jeans open, her head snaps up.

A deep chuckle rumbles out of my chest.

"You," she whispers, her eyes filling with tears.

"Me," I confirm.

Shelby pushes up onto her toes, her lips slamming into mine at the same time I dip my hand into her jeans.

"I can't believe it was you," she pants. "This whole time."

My chuckle mixes with her moan. Easing two fingers into her, I nip the side of her neck.

Always so surprised. And eager.

I grin against her skin.

My hand is rough between her legs.

"I told you not to drink the juice tonight. Didn't I?"

Shelby nods, pushing up farther on her tiptoes. "Ahh." Her cry is one of pained pleasure.

My other hand latches onto the back of her neck, holding her steady as I walk her backward toward the bed. "You know better than to ignore an order."

Shelby shakes her head. "I don't remember."

"Then let me remind you."

Removing my hand, I kneel, shoving her jeans and panties down, when they bunch at her feet, I stand impatient.

It may not have been a year since I last sank myself into her, but it might as well have been. I'm desperate to be inside her. To feel the heat of her around me while she begs me to fill her.

Pulling the baby monitor off the back of my dress pants where it was clipped, I place it on the closest side table.

Shelby lies panting, her ass barely on the edge of the bed.

"In case Riley needs me," I explain.

Leaning over Shelby's frame, I brace my hands above her shoulders.

"I'm done waiting a year," I warn her.

My lips bruise hers with the force of my kiss. Shelby moans below me.

"Why?" she pants. "Why don't I remember?"

I pull away to stare down at her with a tilted head. "Because it wasn't time. You weren't ready. I wasn't ready," I confess.

"And now?" she whispers.

Pushing off the bed, I stand tall. "And now, I'm going to fuck you in a way that will have you feeling me tomorrow. Every time you move, every time you walk, you're going to feel me deep inside."

I watch as a flush spreads over her chest at my words.

I catch and hold her gaze as I lift her legs.

Keeping her knees together, I push them to the right. Her hips twist while her shoulders stay flat on the mattress.

My fingers tug my belt free. My eyes roam over Shelby, taking in every inch of her, from her blushing cheeks to her wet pussy.

This woman was made for me. And only me.

"I will never forget the way you whimpered the first time I shoved my cock into you. I was rough and ruthless, but it was nothing compared to how I fucked you after you came on my cock the first time."

Shelby bites her lip, her thighs squeezing.

I shove my pants down just enough to release my aching member, too impatient to undress further.

Caging her in, I rub the broad head over her wet pussy. Reaching down, I guide myself in. The head of my cock barely pierces her before I pull back out. Over and over, I tease us both.

"Please, please, Leo."

The sound of my name, so breathy and desperate, snaps what little control I have left. One strong snap of my hips and I'm buried so deep inside her that I don't know where I end and she begins.

Shelby's cry rolls into another and then another. My hips swing back and forth, never stopping to give her a chance to catch her breath.

My back arches and my hips flex. My thighs tighten each time I thrust into her with everything I have.

Her body rocks every time my hips meet her ass.

The wet sounds of her body sucking me in deeper leave no room for denial.

Shelby loves every minute of me fucking her raw.

My abs burn and my hips ache, the pain adding to my pleasure.

My spine tingles as my orgasm builds. I need to come, to release inside her.

Nails dig into the skin around my ribs.

"Leo!" It's a cried plea.

"Give it to me. Come for me," I demand, my panted words strained as I fight my own release.

Shelby shakes her head. "Condom." Her left hand releases me to point at the bedside table closest to the window.

My movements slow down as I follow her finger. A stack of condoms.

I grunt. "No."

Her nails pierce my skin.

Hooking my right arm below her bent knees, I lift them higher onto the bed, making room to perch my right knee.

With the added leverage, I fuck her even harder.

"I didn't use a condom yesterday, and I won't today."

Shelby frowns below me. "You knew, at the appointments. You gave me a hard time about couples making this decision together."

Leaning down, I kiss her flushed cheek. "And I'm making the decision for us now."

Shoving off the mattress, I brace on my knee and

other leg, one hand on her waist and the other gripping her thigh. Pulling her body toward me, I cry out at the added force as our hips meet.

"Come. Now, Shelby, come while I fill you."

Two more times our hips connect before the ripples of her inner walls start to strangle my cock.

My orgasm rushes out of me, eager to fill her. Over and over, I pump Shelby full of my seed until it leaks out around my cock.

Her eyes squeeze shut, and she misses the way my body goes rigid, my muscles locking as I continue to come.

"I love you," I breathe into the now still room.

CHAPTER FOURTEEN

Shelby

Wincing, I walk to the front door. The incessant knocking is pissing me off more and more the closer I get.

"What?" I snap, ripping the door open.

A startled Dr. Moore stands on the other side.

"Good morning?" He raises a brow.

"Is it?"

Peering around me, he spies Sam still asleep on the living room sofa.

"Girls' night was a success, I see." He chuckles, and for the first time in four years, I want to slap his perfect face.

Breathing in deep, I tried to rein myself in and tamper down my mood. After all, it's not Leonard's fault.

It's his fault. A man whose name I don't even know.

For the third day in a row, I've woken up sore, sated, and wet. He hadn't used a condom again.

I'd embarrassed myself by going into the local drug store for nothing. And, oh yeah, I could be pregnant with an unknown man's baby.

If he visits tonight, I'm going to kill him.

But even as I think them, I know they're empty words. Not just because my heart flutters every time I think of him or how my body heats at the thought of him taking me again but because of how I found the condoms.

Sliced clean through.

I may not remember what happened last night, but the message was clear.

No condoms.

The same answer as last time I tried to use protection. Only this time, I can't get anything after either. Or maybe I can.

Forcing a smile on my lips, I try not to look psychotic.

"I'm sorry. Morning, Doc."

Leonard's smile falters. "Are you not feeling well this morning?"

"I'm fine. Just tired," I lie.

"Shelby," he warns in that tone of his. The one that says he knows that I'm lying.

I peek back at Sam, who is still fast asleep. Stepping forward, I force Leo to take a step back and join him outside.

"What's up?"

Letting out a heavy sigh, Leo answers without any further questioning. "I need a favor."

"Sure." I shrug.

The smile he gives me cools my heated anger.

"I don't want to leave Riley with Sarah again, but I don't have a sitter. Are you able to pick her up from school and watch her until I get off work?"

"Yes," I answer quickly. No way I'm letting Sarah watch her again. "I'm working the coffee shop ten until three."

"Perfect. Her class lets out at two forty-five, but Miss Lucy usually has no issue keeping the kids longer if needed. Thank you. I'll be home at seven."

He starts to walk away, but I rush, "Wait!" and step toward him.

"If I do you a favor, will you do me one?"

Doc walks back over. "What do you need?"

"Another appointment? I need Plan B," I practically plead.

Leonard's face hardens. "No."

Turning, he starts to walk away.

"Hey, hey." I follow quickly. "Why not?"

He halts and straightens his back before he turns. "We discussed this at your last appointment."

"I'm doing you a favor," I remind him.

"This isn't about favors, Shelby. This is a moral issue for me. The decision to have a baby is a two-person discussion. The fact that you're even asking tells me condoms are still off the table. If he didn't want to prevent it when you had sex, then I won't prevent it now."

"It's my body!" I snap.

"And it would be his child. If he said no, it's no."

I blink back tears. I shouldn't be frustrated since I knew what his answer would be.

At least he's a man of his word. I'm not the only one he's given this speech to. Everyone in town knows how he feels.

"I'll find someone else to watch Riley."

Reaching out, I grab his arm. "No. You don't have to do that. I may think that you're a dick right now, but I love her, and she'll be safe with me."

"A dick?" His words are low and growled.

The sound sends a shiver through me that starts at my head and ends in my crotch. My eyes widen when he steps closer.

"A dick," he repeats, a disbelieving chuckle shakes his chest.

My eyes drop from his grin when he backs away. My eyes widen to the point of pain when I notice the bulge at the front of his pants.

Holy shit!

I did that!

Reaching out, Doc takes my chin between his thumb and forefinger. "I'll be back at seven. Riley will have a spare key in her bag."

At a loss for words, I just nod.

What the fuck just happened?

CHAPTER FIFTEEN

Shelby

Groaning, I lift the brown bag onto the countertop.

"I don't know about you, muffin, but I'm beat."

"I'm okay."

Who knew a six-year-old had so much energy?

I take the eggs out of the paper bag and hand them over to the small outstretched hand.

"Thank you." I smile.

Together, Riley and I unpack groceries until the only thing left is a sucker. Handing over the candy, I throw the spare house key to the side.

"Let's make your dad some food."

Slowly, my mood had shifted. My anger melted away as I continued through my day, until I left work feeling resigned.

On my way to collect Riley, I'd sent her dad a

quick text, but my apology went unanswered. I'd been angry this morning, but I shouldn't have taken it out on Leo.

I can't force my mystery man to use protection, as I don't even know who he is. I'm not traveling to the next town to get Plan B, for many reasons, but the main one being that it's not practical.

The only way I can get it in Cromwell is through Doc, and clearly, that's not happening.

The only thing I can control is myself. No condoms, no sex.

Liar.

I may not remember our nightly activities, but even in the light of day, I know that in the moment, I won't say no. I won't want to.

By the time Doc comes home, Riley has wandered off to her room, leaving me to prepare dinner. The low tones of the radio distract me from my thoughts.

The thud of my knife hitting the chopping board mixes with my humming. In a world of my own, I don't realize I'm no longer alone until large hands slide around my waist while a solid kiss is pressed to the crown of my head.

I jump, letting out a scream. My fright quickly turns to pain. Dropping the knife, I hiss. Bright red blood pools in the slit in my forefinger.

"Fuck, I'm sorry," Leo rushes out.

Gripping my wrist, he pulls me over to the sink.

"Let me see."

My hand shakes, adrenaline leaving my body quickly now that I know I'm not being murdered.

"I thought you were some weird serial killer," I admonish.

Leonard's lips twitch at my words, but his focus stays on his examination of my wound.

"It's not too deep," he whispers, turning on the tap.

Knowing what comes next, I try to pull away, but his grip holds steady.

"It'll hurt," I practically whine.

"It needs cleaning," he explains.

Still pulling my hand away from the running water, I shake my head.

Leo sighs.

Thinking I've won, I smile, but it slips away the minute Doc raises my finger to his mouth. His tongue is warm and soothing against the cut. My finger leaves his mouth with a pop.

That should not be this hot.

"That's disgusting." I huff, but even I can hear the desire in my voice.

Am I always that husky?

Chuckling, Leo slips the digit into his warm mouth again. My eyes flutter as his tongue caresses my injury. Who knew being clumsy could have its perks?

Completely distracted by the way my body has reacted, I don't fight as my hand is placed under the water.

"Keep your finger there," he orders.

I just blink up at him, completely dazed as he moves about the kitchen to collect the first-aid kit.

After wrapping my finger with a pink dinosaur Band-Aid, Doc declares, "All sorted."

"Thanks," I whisper.

Biting my bottom lip, I turn to the cutting board, clear it off, and grab another from the cupboard. Stepping back to the kitchen island, I find Leonard waiting with a fresh knife.

"I'm just going to go kiss my daughter and remind her I'm alive, and then I'll be back to help with dinner."

Still out of sorts, I accept the knife with a small smile and a nod.

CHAPTER SIXTEEN

Leonard

"Did you have fun with Shelby?"

Riley nods, never taking her eyes off the small television.

"Do I have to help with dinner?"

I roll my eyes at the question. I really need to lose that habit.

"No," I answer. "But once dinner is ready, your screen time is done for the night," I warn, dropping a kiss to the top of her head.

Standing, I leave Riley lying on her bed, and the show's catchy theme tune follows me out of her room.

Trying not to startle Shelby again, I make sure to step a little harder than normal as I walk down the corridor toward the kitchen.

"Thank you for starting dinner." Pausing at the

doorway, I watch her chop, her fingers quick and steady.

"No problem." She shrugs like it's no big deal.

But it is. I haven't had a woman take care of us for a long time.

Walking behind her, my hand anchors to her waist. "Thank you," I whisper into her hair and press a kiss to the brown tresses.

Her body responds instantly, shivering beneath my grasp.

Moving to the other side of the island, I take notice of her beaded nipples and smirk. Shelby craves me just as much as I do her.

"I was just going to sauté some vegetables with chicken and rice." Shelby downplays her cooking.

Picking up another knife and a chopping board, I reach for a carrot. "It was a nice sight to come home to."

"Better than Sarah?" She rolls her eyes.

My blood heats at the sight. Squinting, I wave my knife in her direction. "Injured or not"—I nod to her hand—"don't think I won't spank the sass out of you."

Shelby's face flames, and she stutters.

Seeing words fail her, I smirk. "That's what I thought. Stop rolling your eyes."

We chop in silence for a few minutes before Shelby hesitantly asks, "Have you spoken to Sarah?"

I grunt, "I have. Seems her ex-boyfriend wanted to work things out, and in her excitement, she forgot about Riley. Said she only meant to go out to his car and speak to him, but . . ." I shrug. "I also spoke to Sarah's father and the boy's parents. Now, no one is happy." I smirk, proud of myself.

"Good." Shelby tuts. "How do you forget about a child? You should have called the sheriff."

"Perhaps," I acknowledge, "but everything turned out okay, and I don't think McCallister would press charges anyway."

Shelby pulls a face at the mention of the sheriff's name.

"Not a fan?" I ask.

"No, he's given the Cromwells some trouble the past few years. God knows how he keeps winning the election."

"Better the devil you know, I guess."

"I still don't like that she got away with it."

My lips pull at the edges. Why is her being so protective of my daughter such a turn-on?

"I'll charge her double the next time she comes to the clinic. How's that?" I propose.

Shelby thinks for a second. "Is that legal?"

I shrug. "I'll find a way."

"Her mom and dad too. For raising such an irresponsible little shit."

"Consider it done," I declare.

Shelby giggles, drawing a laugh from me.

"Oh, we have cake for after." Shelby points at the fridge. "Leftover birthday cake. It needs to be eaten."

"Thank you." I nod gratefully.

Shelby stops chopping to give me a smile that stops my heart.

"I should be thanking you. The cake meant a lot." Sadness washes over her face. "It's the cake my dad used to get me from the grocery store."

"I know," I whisper with a small smile.

Surprised, her gaze meets mine. "I tried to go buy one, but just couldn't do it. It was the first birthday without him, and I wanted to feel like he was still here somehow."

I can only hope that Riley and I develop the same kind of relationship that Shelby had with her dad. I'm sure the pain of being without him on her birthday wasn't helped by the fact that her stepmother moved out of town a few weeks before.

Seeing her tears build, I round the island and draw her into a hug.

"He was," I tell her confidently.

"How do you know?" She sniffles into my dress shirt.

"Because even after I'm gone, I will never leave Riley."

Dropping a kiss to the top of her head, I relish the feel of her against me. The way her body forms to mine. Shelby's hands grip my back, and she nods against my chest.

"You're a good dad."

"I'll get you that cake every year," I swear.

"That's a promise you might not have to keep." She shrugs, pulling away.

"What do you mean?" I frown.

"Sylvia wants to sell the house. She found a cute place near the sea. I can't afford to buy out her half of the property, so I think the house will be on the market in the next month or two," she states nonchalantly, like she didn't just rip my whole world apart.

"You can't move."

"I'll still be in town. I think. Maybe. Cromwell's expensive." She finishes on a mumble, pulling away to continue chopping.

"You can move in here," I offer without thinking.

The knife in her hand freezes mid-chop.

"I need a nanny and you need a place to live."

"I'm not being paid to look after Riley, so it'd be weird. You're my friend."

I need to think, to fix this. Not wanting to argue, I simply state, "You're not leaving town," in a tone that is final.

Getting lost in our own thoughts, we move about the kitchen preparing dinner in a comfortable silence.

She's not leaving town.

She's not leaving me.

Ever.

CHAPTER SEVENTEEN

Shelby

Helping Leonard gather the plates, I follow him into the kitchen.

"Are you sure all the cake is gone?" Riley pouts, trailing us.

"Yes, muffin. We ate it all." But even as I say the words, I lean over the island counter and drag the cake tray toward us.

A large hand settles on the small of my back, and I shiver beneath his touch.

Depositing the dirty dishes on the marble countertop, I snatch the spoon off the top. Scraping all frosting left in the tray, I fill the spoon before handing it over to the grinning little girl in front of me.

"You're a bad influence," her dad whispers in my ear.

I wink down at Riley and laugh when I see frosting around her mouth. Raising my right hand, I catch the cloth that Leo throws. Gently gripping her chin, I wipe away all evidence of our sweet treat.

"Daddy, can I watch TV?" Riley pleads with big doe eyes.

"I told you no more screens. And it's nearly bath time."

"Awww."

How can he say no to that face?

I quickly find myself pouting with her.

"No." He points at me. "Baby, you can have thirty minutes playing in your room, but I don't want to hear that television."

"Okay," she happily agrees as if she won.

I peek out of the kitchen, shaking my head as she skips down the corridor. "I've babysat kids that would have had a tantrum over that."

"Riley knows not to push. No means no. Arguing will only result in no screen time tomorrow."

"She's a good kid, and she's lucky to have you."

Lifting the plates, I head for the sink, cringing when my core reminds me of my nightly activities.

"What's wrong?" Leo frowns.

"Nothing." I wave him off.

"You're in pain," he argues.

I shrug, "Not the bad kind." *Shit.* I blush at my own words. "Forget I said that."

"Not a chance." He shakes his head. "Where's the pain?" he pushes.

I roll my eyes. "You know where," I huff.

"Your elbow?" He smirks, raising a brow.

"No." I glare.

"Your knee?"

Standing beside him at the sink, I place the dishes into the soapy hot water.

"No."

"Then where?" he asks, tilting his head toward me.

"You know where." I roll my eyes. I don't think my face could get any hotter.

His shoulder bumps mine. "Where?"

"My . . . lady area," I stutter.

Leo throws his head back and laughs.

I smack his arm, not that he even moves. *Jackass.*

When he laughs harder, my lips twitch.

"I'm a doctor, Miss Keen. You can say what it's called," he taunts through his chuckle.

"My . . ." I start but shake my head. "Nope."

"Your vagina hurts."

I pull a face at his words.

"Your pussy aches."

My jaw drops at his bluntness. "Leonard!" I shriek.

I'm so shocked that I don't even react when his hand clasps the nape of my neck. Pulling me in close, Doc kisses the side of my head.

"Have you told anyone else about your boyfriend?"

"No," I blurt, "and he's not my boyfriend."

"If he's leaving you with a good kind of pain, he's your boyfriend." He grins.

"What he is, is complicated," I huff, drying my hands on the cloth towel before throwing it at his chest. "I'm going to say good night to my favorite person in this house."

I feel his eyes roam over me as I start to leave the room.

I'm flirting with Dr. Moore, and he's flirting back! I get laid a few days in a row and turn into a hussy.

It's not cheating if you don't know who he is, I remind myself. So then why do I feel guilty?

A sharp hit to my ass makes me jump. A loud crack sounds through the room. My ass is suddenly on fire.

Doc stands where I left him, a smirk planted on his handsome face, the dishcloth in his hand. "Roll your eyes again. I dare you."

Arousal roars through me along with disbelief.

What has gotten into us? Eyeing him, I feel my cheeks flame more at my next thought. *I know what I want to get into me.*

It's official—sex has turned me into a hussy.

CHAPTER EIGHTEEN

Leonard

Exhaustion courses through my veins.

It's eight o'clock, an hour past the time I was meant to be home. Shelby had been kind enough to collect Riley from school again, and I repay her by being late.

Opening the front door, I step in expecting to find a scene similar to yesterday—Riley content in her room, and Shelby puttering around the kitchen.

Instead, Shelby jumps up from where she's waiting the minute I'm in sight.

"Hey, Doc. Lasagne and garlic bread are in the oven. Riley didn't eat much and is in her room."

I frown at her tone.

Apparently, I'm not the only grumpy one. Did she miss our new nightly routine last night?

Riley had woken up throughout the night. After the fourth time of her climbing in bed with me, I stopped putting her back into her own room.

I didn't have the time to even think about sneaking into Shelby's house, never mind the energy.

My daughter and I woke grumpy and irritable due to our lack of sleep. Shelby should have slept well, but maybe the lack of dopamine is affecting her mood.

"Thank you." I smile, placing my briefcase beside the front door.

I barely finish the words, and Shelby has her jacket on, reaching for her sneakers.

"Hey, what's wrong?" I murmur, reaching for her arm.

Closing her eyes, Shelby takes a deep breath. "It's been a long day."

"Me too," I agree. Catching her chin, I turn her gaze to meet mine. "Thank you for the food."

Shelby softens under my fingers. When she turns to me more, my blood boils.

"What the fuck happened to your face?"

Either the sharpness of my words or the fact I cursed causes Shelby to flinch.

Taking a steadying breath, I ask again, with a much softer tone. "What happened to your face, sweetheart?"

Her left hand lifts, as if covering the red mark can erase it from my memory.

"It was an accident," she whispers.

My gaze follows when her eyes drift to the corridor that leads to the bedrooms.

"Riley?" I ask, shocked.

Absolutely fucking not.

"She was in a foul mood after school. I offered to take her to the park, but she asked to take a nap."

I nod but don't interrupt.

"After a few hours, I went to wake her up. She was grumbling, and before I knew it . . ." Shelby shrugs, gesturing to the redness below her eye.

"My six-year-old hit you hard enough to leave a mark?" I confirm.

"She has a mean right hook," she jokes with a breathy chuckle. "Really, it doesn't even hurt anymore."

Stepping into her, I frame her face. Bending, I press a sweet kiss to the mark on her cheekbone and then another. Her lashes flutter as her eyes close.

"I'm sorry," I apologize. "She has never done anything like this before. It won't happen again."

Confusion swirls around me. Riley is a good child, and she loves Shelby.

"I had to walk away, so I didn't shout at her," she confesses, her voice filled with shame.

"But you did walk away. Riley is fine . . . about to get a serious talking-to and be grounded but fine," I reassure, my thumb stroking her cheek. "Don't leave. At least stay long enough for her to apologize."

"Okay," she concedes. "I'll wait and then head home."

It takes more effort than I'd like to admit to pull myself away from her. Looking back, I see her settle onto the sofa.

First last night and now today. What the hell has gotten into Riley?

My little girl is sitting on the end of her bed, no doubt waiting for me. Her little chin wobbles the minute she sees me.

Giving a heavy sigh, I sit down beside her.

"I'm sorry. I didn't mean to." She sniffles.

"It's not me you need to apologize to, young lady." I maintain a soft yet stern tone. Riley may be sorry, but what she did is not okay. "We don't hit people," I reprimand. "We certainly don't hit people who help and take care of us. What on earth were you thinking?"

My question only earns more tears. Has she sat here waiting for me to get home this whole time?

Stroking the back of her head, I wipe at her cheek with my other hand. "Did you tell Shelby that you were sorry?"

Riley hiccups, shaking her head.

"Then I suggest you go and do that now."

My sweet girl hops off the bed and reaches for my hand.

Shelby gives us a smile that I know she doesn't mean, but the gesture gives Riley the courage she needs to step out from behind me.

"I'm sorry, Shelby," Riley says between hiccuped breaths.

"You were grumpy, and it was an accident." Shelby crouches, offering a hug. "I love you," she whispers.

"I love you, too," Riley cries.

Seeing them like this reinforces the fact that they are the two most important people to me.

Shelby kisses Riley's forehead and stands. "I should get home."

"Noooo."

Shelby and I blink, bewildered as my six-year-old whines and stomps her feet.

"You can't leave!" Riley wails.

"Riley," I huff.

"No, if she goes, she won't come back. I'm sorry. I didn't mean to hit you. I'm sorry, I'm sorry, I'm sorry."

Crouching, I pull my daughter close.

"That is enough. What has gotten into you?"

"Max said that when his dad got a girlfriend, he spent all his time with her, and then they got married, and Max doesn't see his dad anymore." Riley's shoulders shake as she cries. "I don't want you to leave me."

"Baby, I'm not going anywhere," I promise sternly.

"Max said that I should be mean, and then Shelby wouldn't like you anymore, but now she's leaving and never coming back. Just like Mommy."

My heart stills at her words. Scooping her up, I hug my baby girl close.

"I am never leaving you," I repeat.

"Me neither, muffin." Shelby joins, stroking Riley's back. "I'm not your daddy's girlfriend."

"But even if she was, Shelby will always love you, and nothing will change that," I add. After all, I have every intention of marrying Shelby within the next year—right after I get her pregnant.

It takes a good five minutes and many reassurances that Shelby doesn't hate her and that I will never leave before my sweet girl finally calms.

Her hiccup breaths break my heart.

"How about we stop listening to Max Newman?"

Riley nods, her little head rubbing against my shoulder where it rests.

"How about I warm some food up for you?" Shelby offers. "You hungry, baby?" she whispers, stroking my daughter's cheek. "You didn't eat much earlier."

Riley shakes her head, and a second later, her shoulders shake when she starts to cry again.

"Shh," I soothe.

My little girl reaches for Shelby, and before I can deny her, my future wife pulls my daughter from my arms and into her own.

"It's okay. We're okay. You and I can have a cuddle while we watch your dad warm his own food up. How's that sound?"

Riley makes a sound of approval.

Stroking her hair, I drop two kisses on the back of her head. Pulling back, I tilt my head and dip down a second time to quickly press my lips to Shelby's.

Her wide eyes meet mine. Our secret is safe with my daughter facing the other way.

My girl has no idea that this is our second secret. But she will . . . eventually.

CHAPTER NINETEEN

Leonard

The sound of snoring stirs me. Blinking, it takes a few minutes for my brain to catch up with where I am.

On the sofa with my family.

The rest of our Friday evening was spent watching films and cuddling.

Another snore sounds close to my ear.

Turning, I shake with silent laughter. *Riley.* Mouth open, my baby is fast asleep, her body diagonal between Shelby and me.

Raising my right hand, I tickle her chubby cheek. She doesn't stir.

My left arm is dead, trapped under both their heads. The sight makes my heart soar.

I want every weekend to be like this. Just the three of us—at least until there are four.

Wiggling my fingers, I fight the need to move, the sensation of pins and needles stabbing at the limb.

My finger snags in Shelby's hair. *Shit!*

"Sorry, baby," I offer when she stirs awake.

Shelby rolls toward me. "Hi," she whispers groggily.

"Hi." I smile.

The smile that she gives me is shy and sweet.

"I was thinking, you could spend the day with us, maybe spend the night again. See how this whole nanny thing would work out." I try to keep the hope out of my voice. This whole plan of moving her in and marrying her will go a lot quicker and smoother if she agrees to it.

Uncertainty washes over her face. "Okay." Shelby nods.

"Yeah?"

"Yeah." She nods.

I eye the lip caught between her teeth. "Come here." I crook a finger.

Shyly, she shakes her head.

"Shelby."

Careful not to jostle Riley, I meet Shelby halfway, our lips meeting with the barest of touch.

"I'm not working today. How about I make waffles and we head to the park?"

Before she can answer, Riley shuffles between us. "Waffles. Park," she repeats, her words slurred with sleep.

Shelby drops back down on my arm as if she just got caught with her hand in the cookie jar.

Curling my fingers, I grip her loose strands. One good tug and I'm rewarded with a blush. One I know that no one else has ever seen.

"Noted." I smirk, giving a second tug.

I watch as her eyes darken, then flit away.

"The guy I'm kind of seeing . . ." Her words float off, filled with guilt.

"Is complicated," I echo her previous words.

Shelby nods, causing the strands of hair caught in my fist to pull.

"I can deal with that," I reassure.

When her head leans fully on my hand beneath her, I scratch at her scalp.

How the fuck am I going to tell her that I am the complication?

CHAPTER TWENTY

Shelby

"Why do you have to go meet Kaleb again?"

I pinch my lips at Leonard's question. Something in his tone makes me think he wouldn't appreciate me smirking right now.

"He wants my help fixing things with Sam," I remind him softly.

"His relationship issues aren't your problem."

Sighing, I stop folding laundry. "Sam is like a sister to me, so I'm making it my problem. Besides, Kaleb doesn't know that I know," I point out. "Also, you're not supposed to know. I'm still not sure how you figured it out."

Leo reaches for a pair of Riley's jeans, adding them to a pile near him.

"My lips are sealed," he swears, raising three

fingers.

I narrow my eyes. "Were you even a Boy Scout?"

"No." He shakes his head nonchalantly.

Laughing, I reach for one of his shirts. "Sam isn't the only one who's family. I love Kaleb." I watch him swallow at my confession and quickly add, "I love all the Cromwells. They're a second family to me. Plus, if we did this whole move in and help each other out thing, I'd get days off, right?"

"Of course." He nods sharply. I remain standing beside his bed where he sits. We sort clothes for a few more minutes before his deep voice cuts through the silence. "Well," he huffs, "who can argue with that?"

I give him a toothy smile. "I'd better go. He'll be here soon." Bending, I drop a quick kiss to his cheek.

"Shelby," he calls out, halting me in the doorway. "Pack a few things to bring over. Stay a few more nights in the guest room."

Leo might have phrased it as a question, but I know an order when I hear one.

Is moving in with him and Riley insane? Maybe, but my heart pounds at the idea. I can't wait for my mystery man forever.

If this doesn't work out, I'll just move in with Sam. Scrunching my face, I unlock my front door. On second thought, I don't know how fun sharing a house with Sam and Kaleb would be.

Her mom and dad it is. I won't even need to ask. Helen and Christopher would insist.

With my backup plan in place, I secure the door

behind me and head to my bedroom. Might as well get a start on packing.

Lost in thought, I don't hear Kaleb arrive.

"You and I need to have a word," he tuts.

"Ahhh!" I scream, startled. Whipping around, I grab the closest thing to me and raise it, while my other hand grips at my chest. My heart races beneath my palm.

Being the smart-ass that he is, Kaleb makes a quip about how he could have been a killer. Tilting my head back, I take slow, deep breaths and try to remind myself of all the reasons I can't murder him.

Strangely, I'm coming up empty. *That means I can do it, right?*

His chuckle makes me glare. "How did you even get in?"

"The door." He snarks.

I'm going to have to have a word with Sam about her taste in men. Not that I can talk.

"I'm starting to see why Sam isn't talking to you," I quip.

Kaleb gasps, clutching his chest. "You get mean when you're scared."

And just like that, the anger and annoyance leave my body. "I'm sorry. That was mean."

My mind clears. I know I locked the door. Finding the necklace where it hides under my shirt, I fiddle with it.

Is he here?

"I locked the front door is what I should have

said." The words are offered as an apology. Kaleb hasn't done anything wrong.

The man in front of me frowns. "It was unlocked. I'll check the house."

"Kaleb . . ." I'm unsure of what to say. How am I supposed to reassure him that there's no danger when I don't know who my mystery man is?

"It's okay. It'll give me something to do while you finish getting ready." He gestures to the clothes I have on the bed.

"Why do I have to be the buffer between you and Sam again?"

"Because you love me like a brother." He smiles, leaving me alone in my bedroom.

My mind drifts to the last time my man was here.

"Did she tell you?" he calls from the spare room, but I don't answer.

Opening the drawer, I stare down at the now useless condoms.

"I didn't realize that you were seeing someone," Kaleb states, peering over my shoulder.

His closeness scares the shit out of me. I swear the man was a ninja in a past life.

Embarrassed, I slam the drawer shut and lean my hip against it. If you can't see it, it's not there, right?

Wrong.

"Careful," he chides.

Kaleb leans around me to tug the drawer open.

Not happening.

"She told me." I try to distract him.

It doesn't work.

We stare it out, but it's useless. I take the smallest step I can, but it's enough for Kaleb to crack the drawer open.

Humiliation consumes me.

Why can't I have a normal love life? My fingers find the necklace again.

"Do I need to take care of someone?" Kaleb asks.

I quickly shake my head. *It's not like that.* I answer in my head.

When I don't answer aloud, he captures my chin. "Do you need help, Shelby?"

Pain shoots through my lip when I chew a little too hard. "No," I whisper. Desperate for him to understand, I add, "It's complicated."

Kaleb holds my gaze. I don't look away, not even when I feel his fingers pulling the necklace from my shirt.

"It was a gift," I force out.

Silently, I plead with him to understand. To let it go.

"Okay," he relents. "Let's go make him jealous."

"Why would I want to do that?" I breathe.

Kaleb motions to the drawer. "Because he wants you pregnant before you're ready."

I narrow my eyes. "And why would you help me?"

"Because I have someone of my own to make jealous." Kaleb grins.

"Are you going to tell Sam about . . ." I motion to where the condoms lay.

"I'll keep your secret if you keep mine," he proposes with a shrug.

"I don't have one, not really," I mumble, still in denial.

Kaleb rolls his eyes. "You're a terrible liar."

Is this what Doc feels like every time I do that to him?

"You should see a doctor about that."

I pull a face at his words. There's no way he knows. Suddenly, I understand why Daniel and Michael occasionally feel the urge to hit their brother.

Needing to poke back at him, I mutter, "Are all brothers this annoying? I'm suddenly very grateful I'm an only child."

Shoving him in front of me, I follow him out of the house, filtering questions about the Halloween party last week. How does that feel like it happened weeks ago?

My skin prickles, remembering what happened after the party ended.

There's no way Kaleb knows, right?

Right.

CHAPTER TWENTY-ONE

Shelby

What the fuck just happened?

I glance over at Sam, who is curled up in the passenger seat, sobbing uncontrollably.

Absolute carnage. We weren't in the diner for more than two minutes before it took a turn for the worse.

Sam had been upset the minute she saw Kaleb. Facing this thing between them head-on didn't work. In fact, I think we made it worse.

Wherever their relationship is going, my best friend isn't ready for it.

Guilt punches me in the chest.

"I'm so sorry, Sammy." I reach out, squeezing her knee.

Sam wipes at her face roughly with the heel of her hands.

"I hate him," she chokes out.

No, you don't, I silently amend. I'm not stupid enough to say it out loud. Besides, a calm and reasonable response isn't what she needs right now.

Flipping on the turn signal, I pull into the small convenience store parking lot.

Placing her car in Park, I turn to ask, "White or red?"

"Why is he such a dick?" She sniffles. "Red."

I smother the smile trying to creep onto my face. "Because he's a man."

"Exactly," she agrees, pointing a finger at me. "A big . . . dicky man," she huffs out.

The car falls silent as we register her words until my chuckle and her sad laugh mix.

Sobering, Sam whispers, "Men suck."

My fingers find the necklace under my top. "That they do," I agree quietly.

Sam sniffles, wiping at her nose. "Why does he have to be so bossy and all hmmm and grrr." Squaring her shoulders, she impersonates her brother. Although given everything, I'm guessing they won't use that title anymore. Besides, it's not like they're actually related.

Is this love thing complicated for everyone?

"It was kind of hot," I admit.

Sam slinks further into the seat. "It was. God, I hate him." Slowly, she calms in the silence. "Wine and chips?"

Meeting her sad blue eyes, I nod. "Anything you want."

I move around the store quickly, grabbing the essentials—wine, chocolate, ice cream, and more wine.

Too distracted with Sam and getting us home safe, I forgot to text Doc. He must have heard the car because both he and Riley are out front when I pull into my drive.

How long has he been waiting for me to come home?

Waving, I try to hide my cringe.

Peeking at Sam, I let out a relieved sigh, too busy gathering the paper bags at her feet she misses the way Leonard's face darkens. Kind of like Kaleb's when Sam refused to talk to him in the diner.

My best friend was right. It is hot.

Talk about two peas in a pod. Sam and I are made to be friends because clearly, we both have issues.

"Hi, muffin," I greet, climbing out.

One look at Sam's face and Leo's forehead loses its frown lines.

"Didn't go as planned?" he asks quietly as he approaches.

"That's one way to put it," I mumble back.

"Sammy, take my keys, and I'll be right behind you. I just need a second."

Placing one of the bags on the drive, Sam catches

the keys before giving a halfhearted wave to my neighbor.

"Hi."

"Hi." Riley waves back, completely oblivious.

Smiling, I stroke Riley's hair and crouch before her.

"Girls' night?" her dad asks.

"Sorry," I apologize with a nod.

"I'm a girl," Riley states, her look hopeful.

"You are"—I chuckle—"but this girls' night won't be fun for you. We'll do one another time. Just you and me?" I offer.

"And Daddy?"

"Sure, baby." I grin. "Daddy can come too."

"Why don't we have a movie night, and you can pick?" Doc offers, and it's all Riley needs to be back to her happy, sweet self.

"Bye, Shelby," she calls over her shoulder as she runs into the house.

Shuffling closer, Leo tucks his hands into the pockets of his dress pants. "How is Kaleb?"

"I'd say his usual funny self, but he looked pretty devastated when Sam blew up at him. I feel so bad about blindsiding her like that. I thought they'd talk it out. They did not." I cringe.

"They need to work it out between themselves. He never should have involved you."

"I just wanted to help fix it." I shrug.

"Will you be seeing him again soon?"

I roll my eyes. Dr. Moore is not as subtle as he thinks he is. "He's like my brother," I remind him.

"One of these days," Leo starts, bending to collect the grocery bag. Straightening, he snags hold of my chin. "You're going to learn not to roll your eyes, and you won't like the lesson."

My blood heats. Who knew a threat could sound so good? Is it even a threat if I want it?

My body answers for me when my breathing deepens and my eyes grow wide. *I guess not.*

"Don't drink too much," he tuts, jostling the bag in his arm.

I give a cheeky grin at the two wine bottles.

"I'm not drinking," I reassure him. "I'm on best friend duty. We're going to trash-talk men, talk about how awful you guys are. You know, the usual." I smirk.

"Eat proper food and not just snacks," he lectures.

"You're such a dad," I tease.

"Lock your door," Leo orders, handing the bag over.

"I always do."

Yet he always gets in. Guilt chokes me quickly. I shouldn't think about *him* when I'm with Leo. He deserves better.

"And Shelby," he adds, as I'm closing the front door, "you're staying over tomorrow."

Yep, Sam was definitely right.

Bossy should not be that hot.

CHAPTER TWENTY-TWO

Leonard

"Hi, Mom," Shelby answers her cell cheerfully.

Picking up a pink puzzle piece, I slip it into place as Shelby stands. She scratches the top of my daughter's head with the tips of her fingers as she passes.

Riley frowns, staring after her.

Worry churns in my stomach. Am I moving too fast? I look back toward the hall that leads to the bedrooms. Shelby and I have been a thing for years, whether she and everyone else knew about it or not. I'll do anything to make her mine completely now, but I won't have my daughter upset.

After Shelby spent yesterday evening with Samantha, Riley was more than happy to have her attention today. But seeing Shelby more often and her moving in are two different things.

Now I'm frowning too.

"You going to help Daddy?" I ask, tapping the scattered puzzle pieces on the table.

With one last glance down the hall, Riley sighs softly.

"You know you can tell Daddy anything, right?"

Riley pauses, reaching for a puzzle piece. She gives me a slight nod but says nothing.

"I love you, muffin," I tell her, using Shelby's nickname for her.

Giggling, she picks out a corner piece.

Together, we sit at the coffee table, music flowing quietly from the television.

My concern doesn't leave. Instead, it grows with every look Riley sends to the back of the house.

My daughter isn't the only one eager for our neighbor to rejoin us. Glancing at my watch again, I try to be discreet.

"Don't forget it's a secret," Shelby warns, laughing at the response from the other end of the line.

We both perk up at the sound of an approaching voice. *Like father, like daughter.*

"I will call if something happens, I promise. Okay, okay. When something happens," she corrects, rolling her eyes.

I send a disapproving look her way for the disrespectful act. Her stepmom may not be able to see her, but it's still rude.

"I'll tell them. We love you too. Bye."

Ending the call, Shelby sets her cell down, slips past the sofa, and joins us on the cream carpet.

"My mom sends her love."

Riley's little forehead scrunches.

"How's she doing?" I ask.

"Good." Shelby nods. "Settling in well. Making friends. The town is small like Cromwell, so she's used to everyone being up in her business."

"The change of scenery will be good for her," I reassure, placing a hand on her knee.

"I know," she whispers with a deep sigh. "I just miss her."

I squeeze her knee at her wistful tone. "You're not alone."

Shelby's cheeks flush, a small smile taking over her face. Fighting it, she bites the corner of her lip. It quickly turns to a bright smile when she catches my eyes dropping to her mouth.

Shuffling forward, Shelby's fingers cover mine.

"Muffin?"

Riley scratches at her nose and opens her mouth, but closes it quickly. Her right hand scrubs at her face.

I reach over, gently moving her hand away before she can scratch herself. Tucking loose hair behind her ear, I gently pry. "Riley?"

My sweet girl looks between us. "I thought your momma was in heaven?"

"Oh." Shelby looks at me, unsure how to continue.

I nod for her to explain.

"She is, baby. My momma passed when I was very young. Sylvia is my stepmom. She married my daddy and raised me."

"Do you remember when she lived next door with Shelby?"

"And her daddy." Riley nods.

"Yeah, muffin." Shelby smiles, but I see the pain wash over her face. The loss of her father is still very fresh.

"But . . ." She looks even more confused.

We both wait patiently for my daughter to gather her thoughts.

"Max says . . ."

I groan internally at the name. This fucking kid. How can a child I rarely see be this annoying?

"Max says that stepmoms are mean. And that daddies don't love you anymore when you get one."

"Max is very wrong," I stress. "We talked about this, baby. I will never stop loving you. Never."

"Stepmoms can be super nice. Just like mine. We used to bake together and have girl days. She was a very good mom to me."

"But . . ."

Again, we wait for her to continue.

Reaching out, Shelby strokes the back of her head.

"But she left."

"She did." Shelby blinks quickly, sadness clear in her voice.

"After Shelby's daddy passed away, Sylvia was very sad in the house. She needed to move away where she could make new memories. It's hard to explain, but you'll understand when you're older," I try to explain.

"But she called," Riley says, looking between us.

Confused, I nod.

"But she called," she repeats. Riley blinks quickly before chest-heaving sobs leave her.

I flinch at the sound. Kneeling, I reach over the table and scoop her under the arms and lift her over the table top. Pulling her into my chest, I rub her back.

"Her mom left, but she called," Riley wails.

My hatred for her mother doubles. Pain stabs at my heart. Her mother isn't the only one to blame.

My ex-wife cheated, and her lover followed her to Cromwell. She was going to leave and take my daughter with her. Over my dead body, or more specifically, in the end, theirs.

A fact my daughter will never know.

"I'm sorry," I whisper into the crown of her head. And I am. I'm sorry that she's hurting, I'm sorry she's confused, and I'm sorry I haven't made Shelby her mother before now. But I'm not sorry that my first wife is dead.

No one tries to take my child, and no one leaves me.

My fingers touch another hand, bringing me out of my dark thoughts. Shelby leans in close, whispering sweet words of love. Soothing my daughter with me until her tears dry up and her body sags.

"Are you and Daddy going to get married?"

"Would you be happy with that?" I ask before Shelby can even process my daughter's question.

With a shrug, Riley whispers, "Would she leave?"

My eyes meet wide blue eyes over the top of Riley's head. "Never," I swear.

Shelby's face flames. Shock, fear, and want wash over her features.

"Your daddy and I love you." That's all my future wife can say.

"Very much," I agree. "Do you want to take a bath, and I'll read you an extra-long bedtime story?"

Riley nods eagerly. "Extra, extra long?"

"I think we can do that." I smile, soothing my thumb over her crinkled forehead. "Okay," I say. I shift to my knees and set Riley on her feet. "I'll make you a warm milk while you get ready for bed."

Shelby follows suit and stands. "Maybe I should go home for the night? This whole live-in nanny thing might be too much for her."

Catching her chin with my thumb and forefinger, I pull her full lip from between her teeth. "You're not going anywhere," I whisper.

Shelby's eyes flare at my words, and the heat flows into me. She has no idea just how much I mean those words.

"Riley will get used to our new living arrangement."

"It's just a trial run," she reminds me with a shrug.

"She'll get used to it," I repeat. "Let me settle Riley, and I'll make you a juice when I get her milk."

"Oh, I'll get them."

"No," I rush, encasing her hips. Taking a breath, I soothe her with a smile. "I'll do it. If it's too early, the milk will be cool. Go chill, and I'll bring it to you in a few minutes."

"Okay," she agrees easily.

She's so trusting. *Too trusting.*

We follow Riley. My daughter ducks into her bedroom, eager to pick out a story.

The hand I have on Shelby's back tingles with every movement that her body makes. I don't want to have to sneak these moments.

I want her to know who I am.

The feel of her body bumping into mine draws me from my thoughts.

"Max is a little shit. That's probably why his dad doesn't love him," Shelby grumbles as she passes me.

I choke on my chuckle. I will not laugh at that, no matter how true it is.

Spinning in her bedroom doorway, she asks, "Too mean?"

Looking into Riley's bedroom, I remember the look on my daughter's face and shake my head. "No." I face Shelby, and my heart pangs. "Drink your juice and take a shower. I'll bring it in a few minutes," I order.

"Yes, Dad." Shelby nods with an exaggerated eye roll.

At this point, she's just trying to piss me off. It's working, and something she'll pay for later.

"I'm definitely not your dad," I mutter, watching her slip into her room.

CHAPTER TWENTY-THREE

Leonard

The bedroom door glides open silently, my bare feet sinking into the cream carpet as I enter the guest bedroom—Shelby's room . . . for now.

I feel my cock stir at the thought of her being in my bedroom permanently, *our bedroom*. I've been patient this long. I can wait a little longer.

The sight I walk into makes my heart pound and my cock rock hard.

Shelby lies on her back across the foot of the bed, wrapped in a white towel. My blood heats at the sight.

God, I love this woman.

Spying her bare left hand, I push down my impatience. I need to make her mine. *Soon*, I remind myself.

Chuckling, I close the door and make my way over to the bed.

"You're supposed to be tucked up in bed." I tut.

"Hi." Shelby stretches the word out, turning her head to greet me.

"You tired, baby?" I ask, dropping a gentle kiss to her left cheek.

"Mm-hmm." She blinks slowly.

"Good girl for drinking your juice," I praise.

"You're so bossy," she grumbles.

I smile at the way her brow furrows when my fingers confidently tug at the corners of her towel where it's tucked at the centre of her chest.

Shelby stares down her nose at my quick-working fingers. "What are you doing?"

"Taking what I want."

"What do you want?" she whispers.

Leaning down, I touch my nose to hers and match her volume. "You."

Shock covers her face, then confusion.

I love this part. When she figures it out.

Shelby's eyes widen as I pull the ends of the towel apart, revealing her body.

"You," she breathes.

"Me." I smirk.

"I don't understand." She blinks, shaking her head.

"Yes, you do. You feel it too, Shelby. This thing between us." Catching her chin, I pull her gaze back to me. "Tell me you feel this."

"Yes," she answers quietly.

"Tell me you love this." Her heart beats steadily under my palm.

"Yes," she agrees lowly, her eyes drooping closed more and more with every blink.

Closing my eyes, I breathe her in. My hand moves down the center of her body until I reach my target. "Tell me you want this."

Silence fills the room as my fingers slip through her wetness. Finding her nub, I press lightly until her cheeks flush.

"Yes." It's barely audible, but it's enough.

Closing the space between us, I kiss her heated cheek. Pulling away, my eyes drift over her again.

Shelby keeps her eyes on me for as long as she can, but as I roll her onto her stomach, she's forced to break our gaze.

My cock aches, bouncing free when I shove my pants down, desperate to find a release inside her.

Folding my body over Shelby's, I press my lips to her bare shoulder, along her back, and up her neck.

"I'm never letting you go," I whisper.

Pushing in, I groan. The blanket beneath us swallows Shelby's shocked grunt. Her wet entrance greets me eagerly.

Fuck, I will never get tired of this feeling.

"You hear that?" My lips graze against her left shoulder before my teeth nip. The sound of our bodies connecting fills the room. "You always take me so well."

Goose pimples spread across her back more and more with every panted breath that hits her.

Another moan leaves her at my words.

"When you live here, we're going to do this every day, every night." Grabbing a fistful of her hair, I turn her face to mine, my words spoken into the skin of her cheek. "And one day soon, you'll remember who it is. You'll know it was me who put that ache deep between your legs."

I feel her pussy squeeze at my words.

Chuckling, I slam inside her and hold, grinding my hips into her ass, shoving my cock as deep as I can.

I watch as her mouth opens, lost in pleasure while bordering on sleep. I feel Shelby come beneath me, her muscles tensing even as her eyes close and her breathing evens.

Pulling out, I almost leave her before thrusting again. My bare toes curl into the carpet as I give my all.

Over and over, I fuck my future wife.

Pushing up onto my hands, I lift my chest off her back. Glancing down between our bodies, I watch my glistening cock disappear over and over. The sight has me on the edge within seconds.

I can never get enough of her.

"Fuck, baby." I pant.

Dropping my right hand to her hip, I hold tight, my grip bruising. My thrusts don't soften as I chase my high. The sound of wetness echoes over and over, the smell of arousal clings to us.

Standing fully, my left hand embeds in her damp locks, tightening until her head strains.

The image of her bending to my will burns behind my eyelids.

I'm coming, I'm coming, I'm coming.

"Uhhh," I groan, filling her. My hips continue to move quickly even after my orgasm stops. Her sensitive walls flutter with pleasure.

I keep my eyes closed until I finally leave her body. The sight that greets me makes my softening cock twitch.

Evidence of what we've done leaks from between her legs.

Shelby is the only woman who made me want to try again after my first wife betrayed me. She's never leaving, no matter how I have to trap her.

Reaching over her prone form, I grasp the edge of the bedding and pull, folding it toward us.

"Time for bed," I tell her sleeping form.

Pushing off the soft mattress, my eyes catch on the glass sitting on top of her bedside table.

The half full glass.

Shit!

I hadn't come in too early. Shelby had still been awake because she hadn't drunk all of her sedative.

"You're a bad girl, Shelby," I growl, bringing my open palm down on her round ass.

Hopefully, a delayed sleep is the only consequence.

Fuck!

CHAPTER TWENTY-FOUR

Shelby

Groaning, I point my toes. My muscles protest mid-stretch.

I had the best dream.

Eyes closed, I smile. The way he'd used my body, taken what he wanted. I shiver at the memory of dream Leonard calling me a good girl.

God, it was vivid.

My body throbs as if he's still inside me, a soreness deep inside only a good fuck can cause. Soreness.

My eyes snap open.

I'm sore!

Shoving my hand between my legs, I find what I'm looking for. Dry at the top of my thigh is evidence of my mystery man.

He was here.

In this house.

Oh God, Riley and Doc! My stomach drops.

I practically throw myself out of bed, my legs weak and shaky with my quick movement. My face flushes as I glance down at myself. I never sleep naked.

The last thing I remember is stepping out of the shower, the feel of the soft towel wrapped around my body.

I'd been tired and sat on the bed, just for a second.

Flashes of my dream heat me. Maybe it wasn't a dream, at least not all of it. Had Leo been in bed when my man snuck into the house?

The rumble of a deep voice floats down the corridor, stopping my racing heart.

They're okay.

Everything is okay.

He wouldn't hurt them, I reassure myself, but how would I know? I don't even know his fucking name.

I'm not just angry with him, I'm mad at myself. I hadn't expected him to follow me next door.

I won't risk Riley's safety, not for anyone.

Staying here was a mistake. Playing house was a mistake. This man and his daughter are not my family, no matter how much I wish they were.

CHAPTER TWENTY-FIVE

Leonard

Raising my fist, I knock again.

Fuck!

"Shelby," I call out through the door. I know that she's home. What's worse is that she knows that I know. After practically running out of my house this morning, Shelby hasn't left her house, nor has she answered my texts.

Which is why I'm standing on her doorstep, with a baby monitor clipped to my belt.

I feel like a fucking teenager.

"Shelby!" I call sharper.

My tone does the trick, or maybe it's my incessant knocking that's worn her down. Either way, my neighbor's front door cracks open.

I arch my brow.

"Sorry," she mumbles sheepishly, "I was cleaning . . ." She jabs her thumb over her shoulder.

Shelby's eyes drift to my feet as she shuffles her own.

Cleaning my ass. I keep the comment to myself

"If you need help packing, Riley and I would be happy to help." I smile.

I watch as her face flushes. *Caught red-handed, baby.*

"I, umm," she stumbles.

Raising my arm, I gently sweep her brunette locks behind her right ear. "Why are you running, Shelby?" I ask softly.

My girl flushes further. Locking eyes, I let her see my longing. I want this. I want her. My thumb is featherlight against the shell of her ear, and the brush of my skin against hers lights up my body.

It's only been a few hours since I was last releasing into her, but already the need to lose myself within her roars through my veins.

Our gaze breaks when she bites her lip, drawing my gaze to her mouth. As if the spell drawing us closer is broken, Shelby frowns, leaning left then right to look around me.

"Where's Riley?"

"Watching her favorite show," I reassure. Unclipping the baby monitor, I hold it up. Is Riley too old to need one? Maybe, but it makes me feel better knowing I can step out for a minute and I'll hear if she needs me.

Shelby nods once, then shuffles.

"I just wanted to give you this," I say, with a closed-lipped smile. Reaching into my back pocket, I pull out a white envelope.

The heat in my body doubles when our fingers brush.

"What is it?"

I don't answer. Instead, I watch as understanding dawns on her face.

"Why would you give me money?"

"For looking after Riley."

Shelby's head rears back, as if I struck her. A second later, she thrusts the envelope back toward me.

"You don't need to pay me for that. I love watching her. She's my buddy."

My heart warms at her words. "I know." I smile. "But I also know that you've been taking fewer shifts at the coffee shop, and you need money. I don't see why you can't have both."

Ignoring the money still held out toward me, I take a step back. "What time are you coming over tonight?"

"Leonard," Shelby grumbles.

I chuckle at her tone.

"Shelby," I match it.

Closing her eyes, my girl gives a long sigh. "It doesn't feel right to take a wage. Not if I'm going to move in."

"Well, you will," I tell her.

I watch as she overthinks. "How much is rent?"

Anger fills me at her words. I take a large step, bringing myself even closer to her than before. "If you think I'm going to let you pay for anything in that house, you are sadly mistaken."

Shelby blinks, her neck strained as she looks up at me.

"The only thing you have to worry about is helping me raise Riley. I want her happy and healthy."

With a few siblings, I silently add.

"No." She shakes her head, wiggling the enclosed money.

I blink at her.

"What do you mean, no?"

Something in my tone makes her look up from her extended hand. Disbelief maybe.

"Oh." Her mouth twitches. "No, thank you?" The uncertainty in her voice makes it sound like a question.

"You will take the money, Shelby."

"It feels wrong," she mumbles.

I frown at her words.

"I'd live with you for free, no bills, no rent, and you'd pay me? What's the catch?"

"No catch." I smirk. "You'll also leave your coffee shop job whenever you're ready. I'll make sure that you have more than enough money."

"Leo . . ."

I shiver at the way she says my name.

"Shelby . . ." I start, my voice husky and deep,

"The minute that you agreed to try this, you became mine. I take care of what's mine."

Her brow furrows.

I continue before she can argue. "If it makes you feel better, I would do the same for my girlfriend or wife, but instead of a wage, we'd call it an allowance. I take care of what's mine. And make no mistake, the minute you agreed to this, you became mine." Taking care of her is not something I'm willing to compromise on.

I let my tone and expression tell her just that.

"Thank you," she relents reluctantly. "We'll revise later," she rushes, slipping the money into her back pocket without opening it. Probably best, no doubt my girl would argue about the two thousand tucked inside.

I grin at her hushed words. "We will not." I shut her down.

Shelby's eyes widen. Seems she hadn't meant to argue out loud.

God, I love the way she challenges me.

"You never answered. What time are you coming home?"

My cock twitches. *Home.* That's what Riley and I will be for her.

Shelby's mouth twitches. "I'm staying here tonight, if that's okay?"

I tamp down my frustration at her pulling away. She asked for approval, so that's something.

"Why?" I ask softly.

Her cheeks flush.

Does she remember last night? *No.* If Shelby knew who I truly was, her reaction would be bigger. Worse.

If my girl needs time, then I'll give it to her, for now.

"Okay." I nod.

Reaching out, I capture her chin, holding her gaze.

"Go to bed early. No staying up late to second-guess what this is. And drink your juice before bed, all of it."

A smile creeps onto her lips at my words. When she doesn't respond, I raise a brow.

Shelby nods. My thumb moves from her chin to press the centre of her bottom lip, pulling it down.

My eyes are glued to her mouth as I release it. Her tongue sneaks out to wet her lip. The tip brushes my thumb, and my pants grow tight.

Fuck me.

"Yes, Sir," she whispers.

"Good girl," I praise.

It's physically painful as I force myself to step away. I can't wait to have her forever.

I'm running out of patience and self-control.

"I put some flat packs in your garage. Pack at least five boxes." I keep my eyes on her as I retreat over the boundary lines.

"Yes, Sir." Shelby's words are lost in the distance between us. Quiet, they drift away with the winter wind, but my eyes catch it.

Her obedience warns me. I crave it more than anything.

Soon.

CHAPTER TWENTY-SIX

Shelby

Groaning, I look from left to right. Where do I even start? It's not just my life I'm packing up.

When she moved, my stepmother left most of my father's personal possessions for me, saying that the memories of him were enough. Her packed car had held only one box of his items.

At the time, I'd been grateful. It had felt like he was still here. Now, his things are just another stark reminder of how alone I am.

I rub at the ache in my chest.

A harsh breath puffs out my cheeks. Decision made. Dad's stuff stays where it is, at least for one more night.

I glare at the small pile of unopened bills on the hall table and the envelope next to them. I still haven't looked at what Doc paid me. Hopefully, it'll be enough to catch up on one of the bills.

It will.

I bite my lip and force myself to turn away. I may not know the man as well as I should, given our new arrangement, but I know him well enough to know that whatever is inside that envelope is far too generous.

His earlier words echo in my head. *"I take care of what's mine."*

My core heats. *Get a grip, Shelby!* The man meant that you're his employee.

I jump, grasp the cord hanging from the ceiling, and pull, causing the loft hatch to lower. Grasping the other cord that falls, I pull that to release the ladder. As my feet land on the first step, I feel a small twinge between my legs, one that takes my breath away.

Here I am, fantasizing about my neighbor, while still sore from lying with another man just last night.

Guilt floods me.

Leonard doesn't deserve that. He's a good man. Generous and loving.

No. This arrangement is strictly business, at least until my mystery man looses interest. My earlier guilt is replaced with sorrow.

I don't want it to end. Just the sneaking around, lying, never knowing when he'll come for me. Tilting my head back, I groan.

God, I have issues.

My mother's things have sat where they are for as

long as I can remember. Next to the beam, near the wall connecting to Doc's house.

Some things I am willing to get rid of, but my mother's items are not one of them. They come with me. As I get closer, more boxes appear.

Maybe not all of them.

I make a mental note to ask Kaleb if there's any storage room at the trucking yard that I can rent next time I see him. If not, he has a garage, and the man owes me after that breakfast fiasco.

I really should check in with Sam. I'm a terrible friend. But she hasn't called me either, which usually means they made up. The image of them sitting across from me in the diner calms my worry. The way Kaleb had looked at my best friend, the way his fingers had played with her hair—something tells me she'd prefer me not to call for a while.

I'll give her a few more days.

Chuckling, I sit next to the boxes. Carrying these down counts as packing five boxes, right? Pointing, I count quickly. Twelve. That definitely counts in my book . . . but not in Leo's.

I check the time on my watch. It's getting late. Pulling out a photo album, I shuffle along the floorboard. After a quick flip through this, I'll take half the boxes down before packing up my room.

If I get up early enough, maybe I can take Riley to school. I missed her today. I missed him too.

Leaning back heavily, I open the leather-bound

book in my lap. A startled squeak rips out of my throat when the wall behind me shifts.

Letting out a relieved giggle, I place a hand over my pounding heart.

Fuck!

I give a breathy laugh and turn.

My relieved smile fades quickly. *Shit*, I definitely don't have the money to be breaking things.

Cringing, I touch the askew wall panel. The wood wobbles under my palm. Frowning, I try to peer into the crack, but the pitch-blackness gives nothing away. The light filtering in from my hallway is not bright enough to illuminate that far in.

Grabbing my phone out of my jeans pocket, I turn on the flashlight and aim it into the gap. Boxes line the wall, much like the ones I'm sitting next to.

As I push the panel more, something clicks in my head. The panel moves easily with one good push, like it's used to it. Nothing squeaks, and nothing catches. It just opens.

My stomach knots.

Dread settles in every part of my body. My knees feel like they're weighted with stone as I crawl through the opening. My body is stiff as I sit back on my heels. My heart squeezes.

I'm not in my house anymore.

I blink quickly, but my vision swims.

I'm not in my house anymore.

Feeling around the floorboards, I search for my fallen phone.

I'm not in my house anymore.

Shining the light around myself, I see a dust void, a path that's been walked often and recently.

I'm not in my house anymore.

Pushing to my feet, I trace the steps to the attic hatch. It has a latch similar to mine that can be opened from either side.

I'm not in my house anymore.

Releasing the latch, I move around to take the first step down.

I'm not in my house anymore.

The hallway is empty. The sounds of a child's television show drift out of Riley's closed bedroom door.

I'm not in my house anymore.

Someone moves around the kitchen, and the fragrance of what they're cooking reminds me that I skipped lunch and dinner. I'd been too guilty about my unknown man entering Doc's house last night to eat.

I'm not in my house anymore.

My feet feel like they're lined with lead. Every step I take is heavy. Something to my left catches my eye, and I turn. Physical pain pierces my heart.

I'm not in my house anymore.

A family photo. One I've walked past dozens of times, but I've never been this close. Leaning in, I blink to clear my watery vision. My fingers find the necklace under my T-shirt the same time my eyes find it in the photo.

I'm not in my house anymore.

It's his mother's. I'm wearing his mother's locket.

The final piece of the puzzle falls, right there for me to see. How did I miss this?

I'm not falling in love with two men.

There's only one.

I'm so fucking stupid.

CHAPTER TWENTY-SEVEN

Shelby

My body moves on autopilot, my socked feet silent against the carpet. Before I know it, I'm standing in the kitchen doorway.

Leonard stands at the kitchen island, oblivious to my presence. My rage increases with every chop of the knife his hand makes until I can't take it anymore.

"Have you lost your fucking mind?"

His head snaps up. I don't know if it's the anger in my voice or the rage vibrating from my body that clues him in, but one look at his face, and I know that he knows.

A calmness passed over his face.

"Where did you come from?"

Instead of answering aloud, I point at the ceiling.

My labored breathing is obnoxiously loud. His calm demeanor pisses me off more.

Gently, he places the sharp knife next to the chopping board. The room stays silent, and our gaze locks as he reaches up to remove his dark-rimmed glasses. They're placed on the other side of the wooden board.

"Watch your tone."

I shiver.

I find out he's my mystery man, and that's what he has to say?

"You fucking asshole," I whisper, barely holding my tears in.

Leo's face darkens.

"Watch your mouth while you're at it." His eyes flick to the wall beside me that hides the hall.

Riley.

Closing my eyes, I take a deep, calming breath.

Nope, not helping.

I'm shaking by the time I open my eyes, the glint of the knife drawing my attention.

A deep chuckle penetrates the tension between us.

"You thinking of using that, baby?" Leo taunts.

Long, confident fingers wrap around the black handle. I watch, caught in his spell, as he flips the knife, catching it by the blade, his fingers narrowly missing the sharp edge.

Stretching his arm out, he holds it like an offering.

"This isn't funny, Leonard."

His eyes close at my words.

"I do love it when you say my name."

Unable to hold them back any longer, a sob leaves me and then another.

"This isn't funny!" I repeat, harsher.

"I'm not laughing, baby."

And he's not. Leo looks at me with an expression that upsets me more.

Acceptance.

"You weren't supposed to find out like this," he tells me calmly.

"Or at all."

"I was going to tell you. I just wasn't ready for it to end yet."

"Liar," I mumble.

His face darkens again. I'm making him angry. Like he has the right after what he's done. Irritation builds my confidence.

"Liar!" My words echoes out, the space between us closing when I step forward.

"Keep your fucking voice down. I will not tell you again."

My body responds to his threat in more than one way. I really am fucked up. Frustrated at myself and angry with the man before me, I push more.

"Or what, Leo? What the fuck are you going to do? Lie to me a little more . . ."

Before I can say anything more, a small voice cuts between us.

"Daddy?"

Doc and I both freeze. My heart plummets. He recovers first.

"I'm sorry, baby. We didn't mean to be so loud. Go back to your bedroom. Dinner will be a little late."

Wetting my lips, I try to swallow around my suddenly dry and scratchy throat. Taking a shaky breath, I hold on to the kitchen island. The cold countertop helps ground me.

Turning, I avoid looking at Leo.

"I'm sorry, baby," I whisper, kneeling before her. "It's my fault. I shouldn't have yelled. It won't happen again. I promise."

"Why don't you pick out a book? Shelby will come read with you while I finish up in here?"

Her pretty eyes flit to the man behind me.

Stroking my thumb across her cheek, I nod because what else is there to say? I may be caught between wanting to punch her dad in the face and needing to kiss him, but none of this needs to play out in front of her.

When the little girl hesitates, her dad adds, "She'll be in, in a second."

Relief and annoyance mix within me. I don't want to fight with him, but who is he to decide that this conversation is over?

This is entirely his fault.

The kitchen stays silent except for the gentle patter of small feet heading down the hallway. I stay kneeling even after she's out of earshot.

A presence behind me straightens my back.

The room blurs before I close my eyes. When I stand, a sniff gives away my distress.

"Enough." A heavy hand rests on my waist. "You will go spend time with Riley until I come fetch you both for dinner."

I shake my head.

Air catches in my throat. *How the fuck did we get here?*

Rubbing the knuckle of my thumb over my eyebrow, I step away from him.

Not that Leo lets me get far.

"Shelby," he warns.

Strong hands turn me by my shoulders. Shaking my head, I continue to move away, backing up until I hit the wall behind me.

Large, strong arms brace on either side of me.

"You will go spend time with Riley." I shake my head. "This conversation is over." His tone leaves no room for argument.

I forget how to breathe when his head drops low, his nose nudging mine.

"You will spend time with Riley, we will have dinner together as a family, and then you will spend the night."

I shiver when his fingers play at the collar of my shirt, and a moan slips out when they dip below.

His eyes snap to mine. The slight smirk riles me.

He owns me, and he knows it.

Asshole.

The necklace tickles as it slides against my skin.

Once his mother's locket is out of my shirt, he closes his hand around it.

"When Riley's in bed, you will take a shower and wash this anger away. What's done is done. Once you've calmed, you're going to come to me. My bed. Where you'll ride me like I'm your whole world. I didn't intend for you to figure the truth out on your own, and for that, I am sorry. But you are mine, Shelby."

My tummy flutters at the way he punctuates that one word. He really fucking means it.

"Mine."

I shake my head. "I don't want this."

"Now, who's a liar?"

I am.

CHAPTER TWENTY-EIGHT

Leonard

The letters on the page blur. At this point, I'm not even pretending to read.

Shelby went for a shower forty minutes ago, and no matter how much I strain my ears, there's no way to hear if she's done or not.

Insisting on using what had been her bathroom had given her the space she needed to step away, and it's killing me. Only the fact that she's still in my house is keeping me rooted in bed, waiting impatiently.

Sighing, I eye the bedside clock again.

I'll give her a few more minutes.

Movement outside my bedroom door snaps my head to the left. Warmth fills me. That's my girl.

Shelby couldn't enter the room more slowly, even

if she tried. I have to roll my lips to stop myself from smiling.

When she turns to close the door, all humor vanishes, and my cock swells.

The white dress shirt, my shirt, that I left on the spare bed for her, hangs open, falling to mid-thigh.

Her movements are self-conscious, a shy blush blooming on her face. My eyes trace it as it spreads down her slim neck, hidden behind the cotton now clutched in her hands.

"Good girl."

My words have an immediate effect. Her back straightens, and the death grip she has on the shirt loosens.

I pull back the covers.

Shelby stills beside me, next to the bed.

"I told you what I want." My voice is husky with arousal.

Her tongue peeks out to wet her lips, ripping a groan from my chest. The desperate sound spurs my girl on.

The sides of the dress shirt fall apart, teasing me with what lies beneath. My roaming eyes go unnoticed as Shelby stares at my growing arousal. Straining and large, I ache for her.

"Come here, baby," I urge her.

Taking my outstretched hand, Shelby climbs onto the bed, both of her knees balancing on the edge.

"Here," I insist, tugging her closer.

Her throat bobs when she throws her leg over my

hips to straddle me. Unable to wait any longer for the feel of her, I press her hips to mine. My large hands squeeze her waist.

I need to calm down. I'm not even inside her, and I'm ready to come. We may have had sex a dozen or so times in the past, but this may as well be the first time for her.

The first time she came to me.

The first time she'll take charge.

The first time she'll remember.

The shirt bunches under my palm. Fisting it, I pull the two sides apart, revealing her secrets beneath.

The wet heat against my cock intensifies.

Shelby might be shy, but she wants this as much as I do. She always does.

"Fuck me," I groan.

"I . . . I don't know what to do," she whispers.

"You belong in this house, in this family, in this bed."

Her chest rises and falls with rapid breaths. Excitement and fear pour out of her so thick that I can almost taste it.

Placing my palm between her breasts, I whisper, "I belong to you, just as you belong to me. No more pretending, no more hiding."

My hand slides down the front of her body, the muscles of her tummy quiver beneath her skin. Both hands grip her hips, and I roughly pull her, rubbing her against where I want her the most.

Panted breaths fill the space between us.

My hands release her long enough to dive beneath the shirt. The cotton tickles my forearms as my hands smooth up her sides, revealing more of her as I travel up. "Come on, baby. Take me," I urge.

With tentative hands, Shelby grasps my heavy cock. The heat of her slick opening is almost unbearable. Gritting my teeth, I concentrate on not coming.

Shelby cries out, pain and pleasure clear. She bucks, but I keep her seated, our hips flush.

"Fuck!" I hiss.

Panting, we stare at each other while her body relaxes.

"Ride me."

All flushed cheeks and hooded eyes, Shelby is a sight I'd kill for. No man will ever witness her like this.

"You're fucking perfect," I tell her.

Using the grips I have on her ribs, I lift Shelby off my cock before pushing her back down.

"Urgh!" Shelby's head tilts back.

I move her again.

"Leo!"

Hearing my name leave her lips in such a desperate plea has me on edge. Panting, she meets my gaze.

"Ride me," I order again.

And that's all it takes.

I watch her body move over mine, my eyes dropping to where her body grips me so greedily.

Over and over, Shelby bounces on my hips in

small, hard strokes—unsteady and unpracticed movements.

The sound of our bodies joining mixes with pants and desperate cries. Her volume rises with her pleasure, and as it reaches its peak, I'm spellbound.

Crying out, Shelby seeks out my gaze. Mouth agape, she looks at me in panic.

"You're almost there. Keep going."

Despite my words, I move her body for her. My thumbs sit under her breasts, my fingers tight on her ribs as I pull her body up and down on my shaft.

Unable to resist, my hips meet hers on their way down. The slamming of our joining drowns out every other noise.

"Leo, Leo, Leo."

If I thought Shelby crying out my name was erotic, the way she chants it as a plea for more is downright sinful.

And it pushes me over the edge, fraying any hold I had.

Grunting, I pump my hips up into her over and over, fast with no rhythm. Joining me, Shelby plants her hands on my chest, pushing her hips back and forth, riding my cock and her orgasm.

Her locket sways between us.

Finally, we come to a stop.

Wetness pools where we remain connected. What I wouldn't give to get her pregnant.

A sniff sounds above me. My eyes snap up.

Crying, my girl is crying.

The heel of her hand digs into my sternum. "Why couldn't you just tell me? I've been beating myself up all day thinking some mystery man broke in last night and how dangerous it could have been . . ."

Shelby blinks, causing a few tears to break free.

Guilt settles thick in my chest. I waited too long to tell her. Then something else settles with it.

Fear.

She can't leave. I won't allow it. Pain spears my chest at the thought of losing her.

Pushing my back off the headboard, I surge to my knees and drop her to the bed. Splayed out in front of me, Shelby looks up, bewildered.

"I told you, that conversation is over."

Her face softens, but tears continue to escape.

"Don't look at me like that. Like you don't know me," I answer her unspoken question.

I don't say anything else. Fisting my wet cock, I eye the cum leaking out of her. Smirking, I shove my cock back inside her. My hiss and her groan sound out.

She needs a reason to stay . . . so I'll give her one.

CHAPTER TWENTY-NINE

Leonard

A deep part of my soul thrills as I walk out of the en suite behind Shelby. She has a slight limp in her walk.

My girl's sore.

I don't even try to hide the satisfaction I feel. After tonight, there will be no doubt about who she belongs to.

The anxiety and doubt have been fucked right out of her.

Several rounds of sex and eight orgasms seemed to have done the trick. Glancing down at my stirring arousal, I know we're going for double numbers.

Shelby practically falls into bed.

Lying on her stomach with her legs slightly spread is just too much temptation. Instead of pulling the blanket over her naked body, I climb onto the bed with her.

Feeling me close, Shelby looks over her shoulder and opens her eyes.

"I still want you," I admit, kissing her lips.

"How?"

My smile at her mumbled question turns into a chuckle when my fingers probe between her legs, finding her wet and ready.

"I'm too tired to move."

"I know." I kiss her cheek. "Go to sleep."

Shelby frowns.

"It won't be the first time that I've fucked you while you're asleep."

The hips under mine shift, her legs scissoring.

That's my girl.

"Tell me you want this," I whisper against her ear.

"Yes."

I barely hear her answer.

"Tell me you want me."

Her answer is lost, caught between her lips when her teeth sink into the pillow beneath her at the same time as I sink into her.

Shelby turns her head, resting her cheek on the pillow.

Lying my body over hers, I entwine our fingers. Soft puffs of air hit our hands. Little pants that slowly grow steady.

A few minutes later, Shelby's body lies completely still below mine. My blood itches in my veins.

Fuck.

Pushing up, I prop myself above her and swing my hips harder, faster. I watch where we connect, her body growing wetter even in sleep.

A tingle zips up my spine.

When I rest my forehead on the side of her head, her brown hair tickles my nose. Her body shifts as I pound into her.

With a roar, I come in a hurry, filling her again.

After pulling out, I drop to the bed beside her, trying to catch my breath. Pushing out a hard sigh, I turn to take in the sight of her, finally in my bed. My wet cock twitches where it lies on my hip.

We're definitely not done for the night.

CHAPTER THIRTY

Shelby

The feel of the cotton wool in my fingers gives me a full-body shiver.

Urgh, gross.

But even as the feeling spreads over me, I don't stop rolling it between my fingers.

The past few days have been . . . something else.

A deep blush spreads across my cheeks. We've barely left the house, and when we did, Leo was attached to my hip. Hell, we didn't need to leave the house for that to be the case. The man has been all over me.

Not that I'm complaining.

There's that blush again.

Dropping to cotton wool, I scrub my face. Being

in our own little bubble has been everything I could have ever wanted, but it's not real.

We have to leave eventually.

A giggle drifts down the hall, piercing my thoughts.

But not today.

My hands shake as I collect what I came in the bathroom for.

The sight that greets me in the living room makes me fall more and more. These two people own me.

Leo's eyes crack open at my laugh.

"You still glad you joined girls' night?" I ask.

Meeting my gaze, he whispers, "Best night ever."

"I got nail polish remover." I hold up the bottle in my hand.

"Thank you."

"Awww," Riley moans.

"Sorry, baby. Daddy can't have his fingernails painted at work. Even if you did do an amazing job," he acknowledges. Lifting his hand, he spreads his fingers, tilting them to admire our work.

Pink nail polish covers his nail and the skin surrounding them.

"True." I nod. "But I didn't hear anything about toenails." Lifting a brow, I plant the seed.

Riley's face lights up. She has her dad's socks off before he can even register what I said.

Leo lifts his head off the back of the sofa to squint at me.

Putting a finger in the middle of his forehead, I push it back down. "Don't mess up your face mask."

"I want mine!"

"Riley, that's not how we ask for things, is it?" her dad corrects.

Sitting at his feet, Riley pouts, her eyes flicking from Leo to me. "Please, can I have one?"

"Sure, baby." I squeeze her chin. "Which one do you want?" I ask, holding up two packets.

Riley points at the gold packet in my right hand.

Pulling out the slimy mask, I gently lay it across her small face.

"Careful of the bottle," I warn when the nail polish in her hand starts to tilt.

Grabbing the other mask, I put on my own. Together, Riley and I get to work. She massacres her father's toenails while I clean his hands.

"By the time we're done with you, you won't look a day over forty," I tease.

Leo's eyes snap open. "Woman, I'm thirty-eight."

"Oh." I frown, trying to swallow my smile. "Well, you have a stressful job." I shrug.

His fingers capture my index finger. The pout he gives me is the exact one his daughter gave him a few minutes ago.

"I'm going to need another face mask," he mumbles around his pout.

I raise a cheeky brow. "Is that how we ask for things?"

"When you're old and wrinkly, yes," he sasses back.

"Please." I roll my eyes. "Like you don't know you're attractive. You have a town full of women after you."

"I only want you after me."

I look away at his confession, focusing on cleaning the polish again.

"Hey," he whispers, stilling my hands. "Only you."

Biting my lip, I fight the smile that tries to take over my face.

"Daddy, stop wiggling your toes," Riley grumbles.

My smile wins.

I watch as she captures his big toe.

My chest hurts, and I have to tear my eyes away from her.

Longing.

I want this. To be a part of this family.

As my eyes find Leonard's, I know without a doubt that it doesn't matter what he did, the lies he told, and the breaking in, there isn't a single thing that he could do that would make me love him any less.

Leo doesn't have to watch every move I make. He doesn't have to keep showing me how much he wants me because the truth is there isn't anywhere else I want to be, except here with this man and his daughter.

I love him.

I love her.

I love us.
No matter how we got here.

I love us.
No matter how we got here.

CHAPTER THIRTY-ONE

Shelby

For what feels like the tenth time in just as many minutes, I peer through the door to check the clock hanging above the counter.

Reaching left, I haphazardly wipe the table. Thirty minutes left.

My heart flutters at the idea of spending the rest of the day with Riley and Leo.

Heat spreads across my face. That man is something else. I've never wanted a shift to end so badly, but money is money, and despite what my neighbor says, he can't pay for everything.

"Bye, Shelby."

Lifting my head, I smile and wave to the couple leaving. Moving over to their table, I pocket the tip of three crumpled-up dollar bills and stack their empty cups.

"Nice to see you without that new family of yours. I didn't think I'd ever get you alone."

Startled, I drop the white cups and spin. My gasp is hidden by the clatter of porcelain.

Kyle Cooper, former employee of the Cromwell Police Department, stands behind me. Right, behind me.

"Jesus," I curse, stepping back.

Items on the table clatter again.

"Ever heard of personal space?" I snark.

Cooper ignores my words. The way his eyes roam the front of me makes the space between us feel even smaller.

Creep.

"I hear you've been spending a lot of time with that neighbor of yours."

Why is he always in everyone's business?

Breathing heavy, I stare blank-faced.

"Well?"

"Well, what?" I challenge, "You didn't ask anything, just made a statement." Raising a brow, I keep my tone steady even though I feel anything but.

"Ha." He laughs loud and sharp, slapping my shoulder like we're two friends.

Kaleb's right, the man's insane.

Cooper shakes his head. "I thought you were smarter than this, but then again, you're all over the Cromwells too."

I flush at his words.

"They're family, and families spend time with each other, but from what I hear, you wouldn't know much about that."

I regret the words the minute they leave my mouth.

Rubbing in the fact that his nephew ran away last year is below me.

Cooper takes a step closer and snarls. "Fucking murderers. That's who your family is. They killed him, and you know it."

Irritation replaces regret.

I roll my eyes. "The feds said he ran away, and the Cromwells all had alibis. Let it go, Kyle."

His hand grips my arm, his fingers peevish and painful. "I'll let it go when they're all in jail. Along with that angel of death boyfriend of yours."

"Hey!"

We both turn at the sound of an angry man.

My angry man.

Leo ushers Riley into the doorway of the bakery next door before jogging over.

Kyle turns back toward me. "Do you even know what brought him to town?"

"It doesn't matter," I shrug, not taking my gaze off an alarmed-looking Leonard.

It matters where you end up, I silently add.

Visions of my attic flash through my mind, but I quickly push them away. My fingers find the locket under my shirt, the one I still haven't opened, too scared of what I'll find. Cooper's eyes drop to the movement.

I still can't believe Leonard is my mystery man. But I'm not unhappy about it. I feel a tinge as I step around Cooper, a reminder of just how close Leo and I have been the past few days.

The grip on my arm pulls me back against the table.

"He gave you a necklace? Gold locket by any chance?" he asks around a cruel sneer. "I hear his dead wife wore one, one which she was ordered never to take off, yet she wasn't wearing it when she left, or so the police report says."

My stomach drops. Cooper is full of shit. It was his mother's. *I saw the photo*, I remind myself. *But it doesn't mean it wasn't worn by someone else*, a dark voice argues.

I let go of the locket, as if it burns me through my top.

Leo gets to us at the same time my boss, Mia, opens the coffee shop door.

I expect Leo to shove his way between us, but he doesn't. Instead, his large hand wraps around the wrist of the hand holding me.

I watch as pain washes over Cooper's face.

"Release her or I break every bone in your fucking hand and arm." The threat is low and powerful.

"Hey, jackhole, let go of her!" Mia screeches, coming over.

Cooper makes a big deal of releasing me and

stepping back. Leo immediately blocks my view of the former officer.

"I'll see you around, Shelby."

Leo stands taller at his words.

"Not here, you won't, you're barred." Mia announces, "And don't think I won't throw hot milk over you if you touch my staff like that again."

Best manager ever.

The threat from such a small woman cracks the tension, and as Cooper stomps away, I fight my smile.

"Really?" Doc asks, nodding to the metal cup of milk in her hand.

She must have been using the steamer.

"You'd be a character witness, right?" Mia jokes back, but I see the way that her hand shakes.

That makes two of us.

"Riley," I whisper, trying to gather myself, but Cooper's words run through my head. *Angel of death.*

Leo is a good man, a good dad, and a good doctor. He's not a killer, right?

"Shelbs?"

The hand on my sore arm startles me.

"Sorry," Mia rushes, "Why don't you head on home. I'll clock you out at the end of your shift."

I open my mouth to protest, but my chin wobbles. Giving a weak smile, I nod.

Large hands frame my face. "You okay to collect your things?"

"Yeah," I answer quietly.

"I'll get Riley and meet you here in two minutes."

Leo raises a brow. "Two minutes," he repeats, pressing a kiss to my forehead.

Biting my lip I turn to Mia.

"Not my business," she holds up her empty hand. "But when you want to make it my business, we'll get a coffee," she smirks.

Small towns, I roll my eyes and smile as I push the coffee shop door open.

CHAPTER THIRTY-TWO

Shelby

"Ahhhhh!"

Riley's scream rings out as I chase her around the wood-chipped area and onto the grass. Steering her toward her dad, I mouth, "Help me."

Leo grins from his place on the picnic blanket. Shooting to his knees, he catches her around the waist.

"I win!" She grins.

"I . . . didn't realize . . . we . . . were racing." I pant out.

Collapsing onto the blanket, I starfish.

"I wanna play tag again!" She wiggles in her dad's hold.

"It's your turn." I wave at him.

"Baby, go play on the slide and let Shelby recover.

Apparently, she's getting old." I don't need to open my eyes to know he's grinning. I can hear it.

"I got it from you." I huff, still trying to catch my breath.

"Old age isn't contagious."

I feel him lean over me a second before his lips brush mine.

My eyes snap open. Turning my head, I check if anyone saw.

"Someone might see."

"Why would I care if someone sees me kissing my girlfriend?"

I turn at his tone.

Leo grips my jaw, holding me steady as he places a firm kiss on my lips and then another.

"Is that what I am?" I ask shyly.

We may be fucking a lot, but other than that first night I found out, we haven't spoken about us.

"That's exactly who you are, at least until I marry you. Either way, you're mine, and I want everyone to know it."

I swallow under his intense stare. My eyes drop to his lips, and I watch as a smirk takes place.

"Come here," he whispers.

Seeing him lean in again, I allow the hand on my neck to brace me as I meet him halfway. Our kiss is gentle and too brief.

Sighing, Doc pulls back. "What did Cooper want?"

"Nothing." I brush off his question.

"What did he want?" he repeats.

"Nothing." I shake my head, tone sharper.

Subtle, Shelby. I roll my eyes.

"What have I told you about that?" Leo growls, tracing his finger down my jaw. "It's rude. I'm not a strict lover, Shelby, but lying has no place in this relationship."

I glare, snapping before I can rein myself in. "Oh, you mean like you did?"

Maybe Cooper's words got to me more than I thought. Retreating in more than one way, I push up off the blanket. Leo quickly joins me.

"Hey," he calls softly.

I hiss when his hand catches my arm, the skin under my sleeve sore from Cooper's rough handling.

"I'm sorry," he says, releasing me immediately, guilt and worry clear on his handsome face.

"It's not your fault," I reassure.

Leo cups my shoulders, his touch even more gentle than normal. Heat travels up my neck as his thumbs brush back and forth.

"I would never intentionally hurt you. I lied because it was necessary. I needed you to be ready. Ready for me, for us," he corrects.

I know.

"Not even if I roll my eyes again?" I tease.

"Not even," he swears, his voice serious.

We stare at each other for a few minutes before he places a sweet kiss on my forehead.

"What did he say, Shelby?"

"He was talking about you and Riley. He was being a dick, so I got mean, and he grabbed me." I shrug.

Leo nods. "That's unlike you, so whatever you said, I'm sure he deserved more."

I give him a small smile.

Strong hands frame my face. "I'm sorry that he bothered you. I'll make sure it doesn't happen again."

I open my mouth to ask how, but the words die beneath his lips. A moan escapes instead.

Stepping into him, I return the kiss. Quickly, we get lost in the taste of each other.

"Daddy?"

The little voice comes from close by, too close.

Ripping us apart, I shove Leo in the chest and step back. Looking down wide-eyed and panicked, I see Riley smiling.

"Hi, baby," I greet too loudly.

Take it down a notch.

"You want me to play on the swings with you?" I try again more calmly.

The little girl looks between her father and me with a grin plastered to her face.

"No." She shakes her head.

"Are you finished playing?" Doc asks.

"No."

Leo and I share a look.

"You and Daddy stay here." Stepping forward, she points at where we were just seconds ago. "Right here." She points, not leaving until we both nod.

"Well, that's us told," Leo jokes. "You heard the girl. You're needed right here." Snagging my hand, he pulls me in close, our chests pressed together. "Right here," he whispers.

Pushing up onto my toes, I kiss him, earning a deep chuckle, one that makes my toes curl. But I'm not about to get caught twice. Leo might want the world to know, but I'm not ready for that. Not yet.

Pulling back, I smile up at him, shy and self-conscious. "I have a boyfriend."

"You do." He grins, thumbing my chin.

Shit, I said that aloud.

My face flames.

"Don't laugh." I pout. Curling a fist, I nudge him in the stomach with it, not that he felt it, stupid abs.

"I'm not." But his words are countered by the chuckle that escapes with them.

Catching his eye, I roll mine.

"Brat." He mock glares.

I grin at my win.

"Come here," he orders, his voice dropping to a deep husky tone while he reaches out for me.

"Shelbs?"

My heart stops. I know that voice. Shoving Leo again, I step back so quickly that I nearly lose my balance.

Smooth, Shelby.

Waving my arms, I save myself, but not before two strong, firm hands catch my waist. Wide-eyed, I push at his forearms and put some distance between us.

Turning, I come face-to-face with a smiling Helen Cromwell and an irritated-looking Christopher Cromwell close behind. My heart is in my throat. My best friend's parents are my second family. They practically co-raised me.

"Helen," I greet, my voice too high.

So much for not being caught.

"Hi, baby, I thought that was you," she greets, pulling me in for a hug. Her arms squeeze extra hard.

"Hi," I breathe, melting into her.

"It's been far too long since you came for dinner."

"It has," I agree. "Hi, Chris."

At my wave, he turns from staring down Doc. "Hi, sweetpea."

I give an honest smile at the nickname.

"I'll come by soon," I promise Helen.

"Anytime. And you know you can stay over even if Sam isn't home."

I nod, gratefully.

"How is Sam?" Christoper asks with a raised brow.

What? It takes every ounce of self-control I have not to roll my eyes. *Fucking Samatha.* I've known the woman long enough to know she's using me as an alibi.

"Good, you know how she is," I answer vaguely.

"I do." He nods. "I'd rather you both be at ours, though, especially if you're worried about being home alone."

"It's okay," I rush, not wanting to worry them. "It's okay. With Sam there, we're okay."

"Good." Christopher turns to Leonard again.

"Oh, um, you guys know Leo." I gesture to him. "I'm the new nanny." I don't look toward him when I say this. I know it hurt. The words even sting me.

"Oh, that's good." Helen smiles, finding Riley on the playground.

"Leonard." Christopher nods, but his brows are furrowed.

"Christopher."

I stay turned away, but his tone shows just how impressed he is.

Christopher's phone chimes with a text.

"We need to head to the truck yard. They need a hand in the office. Kaleb needs to delegate more. This phone hasn't stopped since I told them to bother me instead of him."

Leo stands straighter in my peripheral vision.

Seeing my confused look, Helen clues me in.

"Kaleb needed a break. He's staying at the cabin for the week."

So is Sam, I silently add, the puzzle falling into place. The only reason she'd lie to her family and not tell me is something involving Kaleb. That man owns her, so maybe she's finally admitted it.

A few more hugs are given, along with promises to get together soon before the Cromwells walk away.

They're barely out of earshot before a body

presses against my back. "Don't ever refer to yourself as my nanny ever again. Am I clear?"

Oh, he's mad, mad.

I swallow thickly.

I start to turn, but he holds me by the waist.

"Answer. Me."

"Yes, sir." I practically pant.

The hands touching me squeeze.

"Why did you lie for Samantha?"

I try to turn again, but can't.

"Because I love her, and she needed me to."

A kiss is pressed to the back of my head.

"Good to know. You ever lie to me like that, and I will not be the gentleman you know."

When I stay quiet, Leo stiffens.

"Have you ever lied?"

Our earlier conversation comes back to me, but I don't want to argue.

"That gnome that you have in your garden, the one that Riley loves?"

"Hmm."

"I hate it," I confess. "It terrifies the shit out of me, with its creepy little eyes."

I expect him to admonish my cursing like normal, but instead, he laughs.

"She picked him out."

"I know." I nod. "And I know how much she loves it. That's the only reason it's not been kidnapped and decapitated." I scrunch my face and tilt my head back on his chest to see him throw his head back in laughter.

Looking down at me, he whispers, "Maybe I won't be so careful next time I mow the lawn. Accidents happen."

"That they do." I nod along. "But she loves him."

"She does," he agrees, wrapping his arms around me.

"Maybe we can face him the other way?"

"Now that, we can do." Leaning down, he presses a kiss to my nose.

"I'm sorry I lied to them," I whisper.

"What am I going to do with you?"

I smirk. "Anything you want."

Before we can get lost in each other again, someone else interrupts us.

"Was that the Cromwells I just saw?"

My body locks up.

I hate this man. Cooper walks toward us confidently.

"Mr. Cooper, now is not the time to test me," Leo warns, pulling his arms from around me. "Go get Riley, please. We're heading home."

Dry mouthed, I nod, but my feet don't move. Standing between the two men, I can feel the tension building.

"I don't know why I'm surprised. Your kind stick together, don't they?"

I frown.

"I wasn't aware any of the Cromwells were doctors," Leo responds, sarcasm clear.

"Killers," Cooper hisses, stepping closer.

My mouth drops open.

"Shelby!" Leo snaps.

I jolt, heading to where the little girl is playing on the swing set, but I move slowly, wanting to hear the rest of the conversation.

"Boy, I am not the Cromwells. Do not fucking push me."

I don't recognize his tone. If I didn't know better, I'd have thought someone else responded, but they didn't. My Leo did.

Heart hammering, I head to Riley.

That wasn't my Leo.

CHAPTER THIRTY-THREE

Leonard

I glance over at Shelby again. She's still staring out the passenger window, but the shift in her shoulder tells me she can feel my eyes on her.

She's been quiet ever since I ushered her and Riley out of the park. I shift my eyes to my baby girl through the rear-view mirror. Wiggling in her seat to the tunes from her headphones, she's oblivious to the mood up front.

I frown at the iPad in her little hands before focusing back on the road. Needs must.

"You've gone quiet," I say, placing my hand on Shelby's thigh.

"I'm always quiet."

True. I roll my eyes, irritation flaring. The disrespectful gesture irritates me even more.

"Talk to me," I whisper huskily, squeezing her leg.

Sighing, Shelby shuffles in her seat. Her fingers find mine and play mindlessly, but eventually she forces out, "He called you an angel of death."

I close my eyes at the phrase. *Motherfucker!* That prick has been digging. He was probably a good cop before he pissed off the Cromwells and got himself booted.

Crossing me won't get him fired. It'll get him killed. I'm not losing my family, and that's what Shelby is—family, my future wife, and the mother of my kids.

The Cromwells didn't have the balls to deal with him when he sniffed around them and their girls, but I do.

"Cooper likes to run his mouth." But the vague answer doesn't satisfy.

Shelby finds my mother's locket under her T-shirt.

Twisting in her seat, she glances back at Riley. Happy my daughter is completely distracted, Shelby whispers, "Have you killed people?"

I feel my heart stop. I'd hoped this day wouldn't come.

"I'm a doctor, Shelby," I say confidently. My hand on her thigh moves to find the nape of her neck. "I swore an oath to help people. I take my oaths very seriously, as will you when we marry."

Shelby blinks at my words, letting them sink in.

"What if I don't want to get married?"

I chuckle at her question and squeeze her neck.

Keeping my eyes on the road, I move to wipe away a lone tear making its way down her soft cheek.

"Am I wearing your wife's necklace?" she chokes out.

"Ex-wife," I correct, "and it was never hers. Even if she wore it for a short time."

Shelby lets go of the locket as if it burns.

"Enough. The necklace belongs to you, and you'll wear it as my wife. You weren't questioning us this morning, so don't let Kyle fucking Cooper change the way you feel about me. I love you."

"I need to go home and think."

Frustration fills me. "At the house with me and Riley is your home."

"You know what I mean," Shelby mumbles, her voice shaky.

"No, I don't." I refuse to give her any leeway. She doesn't get to second-guess us. I never intended for Shelby to discover my other secret, but at least this way, there will be nothing hiding in the shadows.

The way she's looking at me cuts.

"I'm still the same man you kissed this morning," I remind her.

"Are you?" she asks in disbelief.

Reaching for her hand, I pull it to my mouth and place a gentle kiss on the back of it.

"Yes," I breathe.

"Leo . . ."

I wait, but she doesn't continue. Instead, she shifts in her seat to look out at the passing houses.

The rest of the drive is painfully quiet. By the time I pull into the driveway, Shelby has stopped crying and wiped her face clean. My thumb runs back and forth on her palm, our fingers loosely linked.

"I have to pee."

I frown at the statement.

"Riley!"

Both of my girls pause in pushing open their doors.

"What?" Shelby asks, confused.

"That's not how we phrase that."

"She has to pee. What else is she supposed to say?" She shrugs.

Riley nods along.

"You're a doctor, you've heard worse."

True.

Rolling my eyes, I climb out and hold the back passenger door, closing it after Riley is out. Shelby meets us at the front door.

"Quick, Daddy." Riley wiggles.

"You were fine at the park." I eye her.

"But now I'm not."

My mouth drops at her sass. Shelby chuckles beside me.

"Don't think I didn't see that eye roll." Shelby smirks.

I lighten at her teasing. Maybe we're okay.

Riley pushes past me before the front door is even fully open.

Tutting, I throw my keys carelessly into a green

glass bowl sitting on top of a side table beside the door.

"Hey, come here," I say softly, catching Shelby by the hand. Pulling her in close, the smell of her perfume flirts with my nose. Will I ever get enough of her?

Cupping her face, I graze my thumbs over her cheeks with a featherlight touch. Her dilated pupils tell me I'm not in this alone.

"I would never hurt you."

Shelby blinks, breaking the spell.

"Daddd," the loud shout is followed by a frustrated rattle.

"That fucking door." I close my eyes. "It's getting fixed on my next day off."

"Go," Shelby urges, "before she actually pees herself."

We hear Riley trying to get into the bathroom again.

"I'll be right back." The words sound like both a warning and a reassurance. Kissing her forehead, I step back, once, then twice. Turning, I head down the hallway, smiling when I see an annoyed Riley.

It's not until I hear the sound of the front door closing that I realize . . . I left Shelby alone with the front door open, her phone on the side, and my car keys in the bowl.

Fuck!

CHAPTER THIRTY-FOUR

Shelby

The panic on Leonard's face when he ran through the front door to see me reversing out of his driveway haunts me all the way to the Cromwell campgrounds, along with the ringing of my cell.

The Jag feels large and too powerful as I maneuver it off the main road and onto the gravel ground.

How does he drive this thing?

I'm extra slow and careful as I pull up to the main cabin. I should go to the Cromwells' lake house since it's not far. But what would I even say? I've fallen for a man who kills his patients? What about his ex-wife? My heart thumps in my chest.

I don't want to ask the question because I don't want to know the answer.

But I do know Kaleb. If I turn up at their house upset, the first thing he'll do is call Leo to tell him I'm safe . . . and maybe start a fight.

Closing my eyes, I lean back on the headrest.

How the fuck did we get here?

CHAPTER THIRTY-FIVE

Leonard

Ending the call, I fist the cell in my hand. It takes everything I have not to throw it.

Fuck!

Swiping the screen to life, I check the location of my car again.

The camp.

This is good, I remind myself. She's safe there. Sinking onto the sofa, I scrub a hand through my hair.

I can't lose her. I won't.

Please answer me, baby.

I wait with bated breath for Shelby to text me back. When no reply comes, I send another plea.

Let me fix this.

A small doll on the side table catches my eye. If I

had someone to watch Riley, I'd go bring my girl home, but I can't, and it's killing me.

When my phone dings, my heart sings.

I don't know if you can.

I call her cell again, growling when her voicemail greets me. The device in my hand vibrates, and I startle so badly that I nearly drop it.

"Shelby?" The question is practically a plea.

Silence greets me.

"Are you hurt? I can get Riley and come to you," I blurt.

"No, no." She hurries, her voice small, the whisper barely reaching me.

Relief is quickly replaced by disappointment. Maybe I can't fix this.

"I'm safe."

"Did you have a key to get in, or am I going to have an irate Cromwell over a broken window?" I don't care about the Cromwells. I just need to know she's in the house.

Shelby gives a breathy laugh. "No broken windows. I know where they keep the spare keys to the bunk cabins. They should probably hide them better."

I smile, but it's small and half-hearted.

"Can you lock yourself in?"

Shelby doesn't answer. Silence stretches, along with my patience. But I wait, pushing her right now won't get me anywhere.

"How did you know where I was?" she eventually whispers.

I don't bother lying. "The tracker on my car."

"I'm sorry I took it."

"I understand why you did, but I wish you'd stayed."

"I couldn't."

I curse softly.

"If I go to prison, they'll take Riley."

Soft crying floats through the phone. Guilt twists my stomach. It was a low blow, but she needs to know what turning me in will do.

"Please don't cry," I beg, my voice cracking.

"I love her," Shelby cries.

"I know, and she loves you too, Shelby."

"I love you," she admits, her voice a wail.

I close my eyes. Her words mean everything to me.

"I love you too, baby."

"Is Cooper right? Is that who you are?"

It's my turn to give her silence, but the truth wins eventually.

"Yes." More cries greet me. "I've only ever helped people, Shelby. Only those who needed it. Hell, some even asked."

Shelby's breath hitches. "My dad?"

"No," I rush sharply. "He never wanted to leave you, no matter how bad it got. He fought to stay with you until the very end."

Pained sobs twist my heart.

"Come home," I plead. "Let me hold you, let me explain."

"I can't."

"Please." I'm not above begging.

But I've lost the fight, at least for tonight. I wait, whispering my love for her, until her cries slow.

"I'm sleeping here tonight."

"Are you in bed?"

"Yeah," she answers softly.

"Do you have a blanket?" I hate the thought of her being cold and lonely.

"Yeah."

I hear rustling and picture her nodding against her pillow.

Twisting, I bring my feet up onto the sofa and shuffle until I'm lying down.

"I'll come to the camp in the morning."

"No."

"I'm seeing you tomorrow, Shelby." I mean it.

"I don't . . . I need time." She struggles to explain.

"I can't give you that," I admit.

Shelby sighs. "I don't want to come to the house."

Fuck!

"I would never hurt you," I promise. "The park?"

"No," she denies me again, her voice shaky.

Memories of our last trip tease me. Okay, probably not the best idea.

"The diner," I counteroffer. "We can distract Riley with pancakes, but Shelby, we won't be talking about my patients in public."

"Okay," she agrees.

"Don't end the call. Stay on the line with me," I whisper.

I hear rustling again.

"I'm going to fix this, baby. And then I'm going to marry you."

Stuttered breathing and a sniffle are my only answers. At least she didn't say no.

I can fix this.

Nothing else is acceptable.

CHAPTER THIRTY-SIX

Shelby

Curling my left hand around my right, I try to stop shaking.

Glancing left, I search the parking lot again for Doc and Riley. My heart is pounding so hard, I wonder if the couple walking past me can hear it.

A car starting close by startles me.

Chill out. I roll my eyes.

I feel wired like a bomb ready to go off, and Leo's the trigger. How can I love someone who's done things that are so bad?

Loud male voices catch my attention. Turning, I see the Cromwell brothers.

Shit!

Stepping back, I keep going until the side of the

building hides me. I squeeze my eyes closed and wrap my arms around myself.

Breathing in deep, I focus on the rise and fall of my chest.

Can I do this? Can I stay with Leo after everything he's done?

Perhaps it's a good thing we can't discuss it openly here. I'm not sure I even want to know. Some things are just better left unsaid.

Voices in the parking lot pick up, forcing my eyes open.

I see Riley instantly. Weaving between the rows of parked cars, she tugs her father's hand, trying to get him to walk faster, her mouth moving with words that make her dad roll his eyes.

The sight makes me laugh out loud. The sound is mixed with relief and grief because I know that, yes, I can ignore what I know. I want these two people in my life, no matter what.

As if he heard me, Leonard's eyes find me. His face is stained with worry.

Lifting my hand, I give a small wave and a half smile. The change is instant. A bright smile takes over his face, and his whole body shifts, a weight lifting.

He knows.

Doc lengthens his stride, and the two approach quickly. I step closer to them and away from the café. Going home sounds good right now.

Riley grins, waving excitedly when she finally spots me.

Everything happens so quickly.

One minute she's holding her father's hand, and the next she's slipped free, running across the lot toward me.

The voices to my right get louder, mixing with music, and I can see a commotion near the entrance from the corner of my eye.

A car screeches, and I watch in horror as it peels away quickly. Tires screech, and voices shout.

My eyes return to Riley, and my world stops. It's coming right at her. My sweet girl freezes.

I don't think. Before my next breath, my body propels forward, moving on its own. I see Leo running from the other side, but he's going to be too late . . . so am I.

Scooping Riley into my arms, I turn her away from the car just in time.

Pain explodes in my leg and hip. I curve my body around the small figure in my arms, trying to protect her.

Pain spreads through me from one place to the next as I hit the windshield and fly off the car. Seeing the asphalt coming quickly, I turn again, putting my body below Riley and stretch my arm out to catch us.

Stupid move. I feel the bone break. My whole body feels like it's on fire.

Groaning, I try to breathe through the pain, through the panic.

Riley! Is she okay?

I try to say the words aloud, but it's like my body

has shut down. The only thing I know is I have to protect Riley.

Something shifts my body, pulling my arms, but I hold my girl tighter. I can't let her get hurt.

Words filter in, muffled and strained.

Leo.

I blink, trying to see, but my vision is blurred.

"It's me, Shelby."

I blink again. He doesn't sound right.

"Let Riley go."

But I can't, my arm doesn't feel right. My body shakes uncontrollably.

I feel my hold on Riley being lifted before the weight of her small form leaves me.

Is she okay?

I try to ask, but nothing happens. The voices above me mesh. The only thing seeping in is the sound of a young child crying.

Riley!

Hands smooth over my legs, and someone grabs my hand, holding on for dear life.

"Riley," I try again, but no sound escapes me.

My body is jostled and lifted. It feels like I'm moving, but I can't focus enough to see. The crying follows, and my heart breaks open.

I didn't protect her.

I didn't save my baby.

CHAPTER THIRTY-SEVEN

Leonard

My world is shattered.

My baby girl clings to Michael Cromwell, and quiet sobs leave her shaking. Her eyes are riveted to where Shelby lies quietly on the stretcher, while the paramedic rushes to start an IV.

But cries are good, it means she's awake. Physically, she looks okay, but I've been a doctor long enough to know that fact means little in situations like this. So if holding Michael makes Riley feel better, then so be it.

A pain-filled groan pulls my eyes back to the woman who owns my heart.

"I'm right here, baby. Riley's okay. If you can hear me, Shelby, Riley's okay."

I pray that a higher power doesn't make me a liar.

I try to listen to the medical talk, but the words fly over my head, all my training forgotten at the thought of losing my family.

We arrive at the hospital quickly, but not quickly enough. The negotiations I've been involved in with Christopher Cromwell regarding the construction of a new hospital here in Cromwell are over. He can have whatever he wants.

We need a hospital in town. Every minute counts in moments like this.

My heart twists again.

I only just got her. I can't lose her.

Shelby is unloaded quickly, and suddenly, my girls are being taken in different directions. I look at Michael; my arms go out for Riley.

My little girl doesn't come easily; we have to practically pry her away. She's latched onto him in her moment of trauma and fear.

"I'll stay with Shelby as much as I can. Come find us after Riley's given the all clear."

When I hold his gaze, he pats my shoulder, and Kaleb is already following after Shelby.

"She won't be alone, I promise."

My soul splits into two along with my heart.

Shelby disappears through the white double doors quickly, nurses and doctors rushing after her. Riley cries harder, her little arms stretched out as she calls for Shelby.

CHAPTER THIRTY-EIGHT

Leonard

"You're not family."

The words echo in my head. Over and over, the nurse's words punch me in the gut. No one will tell me anything about Shelby.

Sitting forward in the uncomfortable white plastic seat, I scrub the back of my neck.

I'll be changing that real fucking soon.

But telling them that she's my fiancé hadn't been enough, not when she's still unconscious, especially after I tried to look at her chart.

She's okay, I try to convince myself.

I'm looking right at her. Lying in the hospital bed, Shelby looks pale and fragile. The monitor to her left shows a steady heart rate. She's been assessed and treated.

I need patience, the one thing that I'm out of.

Pulling out my phone, I text Lara Cromwell, wanting another picture of Riley. The reply comes quickly. Face covered in chocolate ice cream, my sweet girl smiles at me through the lens. The picture blurs.

Sniffling, I wipe my nose.

She's okay, I know she is. I'd insisted on more scans and X-rays than necessary, but when all came back clear, the hospital was happy to discharge her.

I owe Michael and Kaleb. They'd kept Michael's word and stayed with Shelby until they were kicked out of the room, and even then, they'd stayed in the viewing room with some interns.

They'd never left her.

Movement on the bed has me shooting to my feet.

Shelby!

Grabbing her hand with my left, I press the call button with my right.

"Hi, baby. You're okay, you're okay." I whisper, stroking her face with the back of my hand.

Shelby's mouth opens and closes silently; wide, panicked eyes flit about as if she's searching.

"She's okay, Riley's safe. You saved her." I croak, blinking back tears. "You saved her," I repeat, kissing her forehead.

CHAPTER THIRTY-NINE

Leonard

Dr. Webb plants her feet at the base of Shelby's hospital bed, and nurses and a few interns crowd the room behind her.

Giving a quick nod in greeting, I turn back to Shelby. Pale and drowsy, she holds my hand.

Dr. Webb's words feel like a physical blow. "Well, the good news is, your hip's not broken or fractured. That was my main concern with the place of impact."

Good, that's good. I squeeze my eyes closed.

"You fractured your left radius and ulna, but surgery should be avoidable, and I think it'll heal well with the cast. Your shoulder has been reset; the dislocation was sorted while you were sedated. It may feel achy, but you'll be on pain medication for a few weeks."

Shelby's eyes widen more and more with every injury.

I fist the edge of the bed to hide my anger.

How did the Cromwells let this happen?

"The biggest injuries you sustained were the miscarriage and a broken clavicle."

For the second time today, my world stops.

Shelby's head snaps to the left, startled eyes meeting mine.

"We'll monitor this and I'm sure Dr. Moore will help at home, but again I'm confident that we can avoid surgery." Dr. Webb continues, like she didn't just stab me in the heart.

"Miscarriage?" Shelby barely gets out.

"Err, yes," the doctor says hesitantly. She glances at the chart in her hand, then at me. "I thought you'd seen."

"No," I choke out. "Your nurse took it before I could read it. No one would talk until Shelby was awake."

"My apologies."

But it's too late.

"She was pregnant?" I breathe.

Shelby tenses in my grasp. Reaching up, I soothe brown curls away from her creamy cheek.

"Yes. When you were brought in, a test was run, and the hCG level indicated a few weeks or less."

My eyes sting as I hold back my tears. Taking a deep breath, I channel all the professionalism I can. "Did she have any bleeding?"

"A little. I'd recommend seeing your usual OB-GYN for a follow-up."

"Of course." I nod, "I'll take care of her." My thumb wipes at the tear on Shelby's cheek, but it's quickly replaced.

I hear feet shuffling, and the door closes soon after.

"I didn't know," Shelby whispers with a shake of her head.

Stroking her hair back, I kiss her forehead.

"I'll take care of you," I promise, trailing kisses down to her cheek.

Squeezing my eyes closed, I rest my forehead against her ear. Bent over her awkwardly, I wrap my arms around her the best I can while avoiding the sling on her right arm and the cast on her left.

The air in my lungs burns until eventually it leaves, taking my grief with it.

One after another, tears escape, dripping into the curls below.

"I'm sorry."

Shelby's words make my grief grow. She has nothing to apologize for. I tell her just that.

"Don't you dare. You saved Riley. You saved her." I punctuate my words with kisses, then frame her face. "You never have to apologize to me. I owe you every-thing." I kiss her lips, and her face distorts as more of her own tears escape. "I'm sorry I couldn't stop this."

Shelby shakes her head.

"It's not your fault."
Foreheads resting together, we grieve.

CHAPTER FORTY

Leonard

The hospital room has been silent for a while.

Still, sterile, and quiet.

Movement in the hall draws my attention.

Cromwells. Kaleb and Samantha approach hand in hand. Pushing off the hard seat, I meet them outside the door.

I force the words from my mouth, painful and bitter, as I explain about the baby. Kaleb and I stand watching as Samantha rushes to comfort her best friend.

I watch as Shelby's last shield comes down and she sobs, even harder than before, for the loss of our baby, the accident, hell, maybe even for the secrets I now force her to keep.

The sight rips my heart out.

I force myself to tell Kaleb about her injuries; I deserve to say them out loud.

Together, we keep watch over our girls, as one offers comfort and the other seeks the strength she needs.

Samantha is giving Shelby something that I can't right now—peace.

Sounds of crying and whispers dim until the room is once again quiet, and my sadness turns to rage once more.

Cooper will pay for this, all of it, but he's not the only one to blame.

My throat feels like it's closing. "This is your fault." I force out.

"He may have been there because of us, but Cooper's actions are his own," Kaleb argues.

"I'm not talking about the car plowing into my family." Shaking my head, I huff a hollow laugh. "You and your brothers should have taken care of him well before now. He shouldn't still be on this earth to be driving!"

That gets his attention; his blond head snaps to me.

"You've been fucking around with him for years. This"—I point at the bed—"is on the three of you." I mean it.

For years, I've ignored the obvious issues in this fucking town. The Cromwells aren't as sneaky as they think they are, but up until now, it's not been my business. After all, they don't interfere with my extra activities. I tell him as much.

"We'll take care of it."

It's not good enough.

"No, you had your chance." I glare.

"We're Shelby's family," he reminds me.

I let his words sink in.

If I take care of Cooper, the Cromwells will have something on me, and that just won't do.

Keeping my eyes on the bed, I offer, "Then maybe it needs to be a family event."

No other words are spoken on the matter, but the silence says it all.

"Can you stay with her?" I whisper, "I need to see Riley. Just show myself that she's okay, but I don't want to leave Shelby alone."

Kaleb nods. "Of course." Turning away from the sleeping women, he promises, "We'll stay as long as you need."

CHAPTER FORTY-ONE

Leonard

Leaning against the back passenger door, I take another breath, the hot air clouds as it mixes with the winter night.

"Everything okay, Doctor?"

I open my eyes at Duke's voice.

The old gas station owner stands near the back of my Jag, wringing his hands.

"Sorry." I apologize, pushing off the door.

"Nothing to apologize for, son. I just thought you'd head straight off after paying."

I give a small smile. "Just needed a minute."

"I hear it was bad."

More than you will ever know.

I keep the thought to myself. "Could have been

worse," I mutter instead. And it could have been. I could have lost three people today instead of just one.

The thought makes me feel sick.

Opening the driver's side door, I sink into my seat.

"Shelby's a good kid."

She's twenty-three, but I don't correct him.

"No one's come by and asked yet, but if they did, I'd tell them that Cooper was here midday filling up his car." Stepping into the gap of my open door, he lowers his voice, "Had his laptop open with a motel in Rowland up. It's about twenty minutes south on the I-95."

Stepping back, the older man tucks his hands into his overalls and shrugs carelessly, "Maybe I saw the screen, maybe I didn't."

Turning my head slowly, I catch his gaze. "Your eyes weren't too good at your last physical."

"No, no, they weren't." He shakes his head.

At that moment, I know I don't have to worry about the cops, not from Duke anyway. He's a family man, and he understands.

Nodding, I reach to close the door.

"Have a good night, Duke."

CHAPTER FORTY-TWO

Leonard

Tilting my head, I watch the man sleep. It was surprisingly easy to get in here. I expected more, even from this shitty little place.

No security, no cameras, no front desk staff on shift. Hell, even the room lock barely fought.

When I step forward, the light from the thin blue curtains catches the syringe in my hand, the clear liquid ready to be administered.

Midazolam. A quick stop by my office, and I had what I needed.

Cooper's eyes fly open the minute he feels the pinch on his upper arm. Stabbing through his T-shirt, I waste no time plunging the drug into him.

My left hand wraps around his neck, squeezing. My right soon joins.

His eyes bulge, and his hands claw at my covered arms sloppily.

He falls unconscious quickly.

It takes every ounce of willpower to pull my hands away. Staggering back, I pant against the dull wall.

He's not dying that easily.

I have plans for him.

CHAPTER FORTY-THREE

Shelby

"Think you can eat all of that for me?" I ask Riley.

My sweet girl nods enthusiastically, shoving another spoonful of red Jell-O into her mouth.

"Quick"—I smirk, glancing out the window into the hall—"before he comes back and tells us off for eating too many pots. And by us, I mean you." I tickle her belly.

Our timing is perfect. Leo appears at the hospital room door just as Riley eats the last bit of Jell-O.

Sighing, I lean back on the thick pillows and give him a small smile when he enters.

"Hi," I breathe.

"Don't think I didn't see that." He glares playfully. Coming closer, he leans down to press a kiss to Riley's head and then mine, his hand squeezes my fingers.

I close my eyes at the feeling. It's the only way he's touched me since we found out about the baby.

"Right, baby girl. Time to go home." He claps, reaching for Riley.

"Aw. Can't we stay?" she pouts.

"No, baby. You've been here all morning. You have schoolwork to catch up on."

"I'm coming home tomorrow. We can have a movie night," I offer, hoping to calm her.

"Maybe."

My head snaps to Leonard.

"We'll see what your doctor says."

Like hell! After a week of being monitored and tested, I'm more than ready to get out of here.

"I'm going home."

Wherever that is now.

My eyes fill.

A large hand smooths over the back of my head before he presses his lips firmly on my forehead.

"We'll see," he whispers against the skin.

His thumb is gentle as it wipes away my stray tear.

"I'll be back in two hours. Try to sleep while you can." The back of his fingers smooth down my wet skin. "You're not sleeping enough."

"Nurses come in and out in the night."

Leo adjusts the pillows behind me. "I know, baby."

We both freeze at his choice of words. I watch as he shuts down right in front of me.

"Rest," he tells me.

Riley climbs up on the bed to hug me. Wrapping my arms around her, I squeeze her tight, breathing her in.

I press my cheek to her hair, and my heart calms.

"See you tomorrow." I kiss her head.

"Bye, Momma," she whispers. The word punches me in the throat the same way that it has since she's been calling me that after the accident.

I hold her tighter, avoiding her father's gaze.

Words are lodged in my throat. I press two quick kisses to her hair before releasing her with a sniffle.

"I'll be back soon," Leo promises, lifting Riley off the bed.

My eyes stay glued on them until I can't.

Tilting my head, I groan.

I'm definitely going home tomorrow. I can't stare at these white walls anymore.

I fight as my eyes grow heavy, but it's useless. Leo was right. I am tired. Actually, I'm exhausted.

I drift in and out of sleep for what feels like hours. Frowning, I glance at the door.

Biting my lip, I reach for my phone, scrolling through my messages for Sam.

Hi, let me know when Riley gets there, so I know she's okay.

Sam's reply comes quickly.

She's here. Sorry, thought Leo would have told you.

Two seconds after her text, my phone chimes with

a photo. One of Riley sitting happily coloring a picture of a dog. Definitely not schoolwork.

The sight makes me smile.

Thank you for watching her.

Of course, she's family.

Her dad might disagree. I reply.

He still being weird?

More than normal, you mean? Yes.

I chuckle at the skull emoji she sends. Fitting.

When did he leave?

A little over an hour and a half ago.

He's avoiding coming back. Maybe he really is done with me.

Want me to come sit with you? Kaleb can stay with Riley. Sam offers.

No. She needs you more but thank you.

Dropping my phone on the bed, I cover my face with my hands.

Is this how it ends? Because of Cooper?

CHAPTER FORTY-FOUR

Leonard

The smell of damp and stale air fills my lungs along with bitterness.

My shoes echo through the abandoned building. Dust and debris grind under my soles, kicking up to settle onto the brown leather.

I weave through the distressed building, the one I want to knock down and build a hospital on top of.

Kyle Cooper lies bound and gagged right where I left him on the dirty floor.

It felt right to bring him here.

Shucking off my suit jacket, I hang it on a low wooden beam. The bag in my hand thuds as it lands on the concrete floor.

"Let's begin, shall we?"

CHAPTER FORTY-FIVE

Shelby

The click of my room door stirs me.

Hearing soft footsteps head to the base of my bed and the clipboard being lifted, I keep my eyes closed. Just another nurse. I thought it was Leo.

Sheets of paper flip a few times before my chart is placed back where they got it.

I frown. Why aren't they leaving?

Opening my eyes a little, I start seeing Leo in the seat beside the bed.

"I didn't mean to wake you."

"Where were you?" I croak.

A smile pulls at my lips when he reaches for me. I turn my hand for him to take, but he doesn't take it, his hand dropping back to his own lap.

Leo scrubs his palms against his pant legs.

He can't even touch me. For what must be the hundredth time this week, my chest heaves.

"Riley wouldn't settle. She wanted me to stay at the house for a little while."

Liar.

Turning my face, I look away, unable to keep the tears at bay.

I don't call him on his lie or ask him to leave. Instead, I cry.

I love him, no matter what.

CHAPTER FORTY-SIX

Shelby

"I'll walk." I huff, eyeing the wheelchair.

Leonard tilts his head back and closes his eyes.

"It's hospital policy," he insists, catching my defiant gaze. Releasing the handles, he approaches me on the bed. "And even if it wasn't, you'd still be using it."

Crouching in front of me, Leo starts to reach for me, his hands hovering over my knees for just a second before he retreats, resting them on his own thigh.

"Get your cute ass in the chair so I can take you home."

The thought of going back to my empty house makes me want to cry. I roll my lips in and avert my gaze while blinking away tears.

Misunderstanding my sadness, Leo swipes my cheek.

"You're healing nicely. Emile has agreed to travel to Cromwell twice a week to oversee your physio."

I nod at what I already know.

His obsession with getting the best doctors to help my recovery helps a little, even if he can't stand to touch me.

Leonard steps back, allowing the nurse to help me into the chair.

I wave at the nurses as we leave, but it's half-hearted.

What happens now? If he and I are over, do I tell the sheriff what I know, or do I let him continue "helping" people?

I roll my eyes at the word, and thankfully, the move is hidden, and Doc is unable to see it from behind me.

"Let's get you in, shall we?" Justine, my nurse, says with a smile. "Front or back seat?" she asks, her question directed at the man behind me.

I groan as I stand from the chair, the movement jolting my shoulder.

"Front."

I close my eyes at Leo's clipped tone.

"Careful," Justine encourages, her hands gentle yet sturdy as she supports me from the right.

Air leaves me in a whoosh when my slinged arm touches the seat.

"Remember, you have the painkillers when you need them. Don't suffer in silence."

221

I nod.

"I'll make sure she stays on top of them," Leo says, handing off the wheelchair.

I bite my lip as the car pulls away from the curb.

"Will you?" I ask, wetting my lips.

Concentrating on the road, Leonard doesn't look at me. "Will I what?"

"Watch my meds?"

"Of course." He nods, like it's obvious.

After all, he is a doctor. The fact is bitter in my mind.

"No need. I'll come by your office when I need refills."

"You've had an attitude since yesterday. I suggest you either say what's bothering you or lose the brattiness."

Brattiness? Brattiness!

I swing my head to the left.

"Fuck you!"

Startled eyes leave the road, and I let him see my anger just for a second.

"I'm a brat for trying to make this easier on both of us."

"No, you're a brat for giving attitude to the person trying to help you."

"Maybe," I concede, "but you're a fucking coward!"

I blink away tears.

The car stops sharply at a red light, and the movement aggravates my aching body.

Leo catches my chin. "You're begging to go over my knee." But the anger leaves his face quickly when he reads my pain.

"Shit," he curses.

I blink in surprise, letting out a shocked laugh.

A smile tugs at his lips, mirroring my own.

"I'm doing a poor job of taking care of you already. I'm sorry."

"I don't want to go home," I whisper tearfully.

Doc frowns. "Why would you not want to go home?"

I lean into the hand brushing my hair back, a shiver flowing through me when he caresses my ear.

Opening and closing my mouth, I fight to get the truth out. "I want to stay with you. You and Riley," I confess truthfully.

Tilting his head, Leo pulls back, looking confused. A breathy chuckle leaves him. Relief and disbelief.

Knocking my chin gently, he asks, "Where else would you be?"

A car horn behind startles me.

Raising a hand in apology, Leonard presses the gas.

Frowning, I worry my lip. "You won't touch me," I whisper so low that even I barely hear the words.

Doc draws in air as if to respond, but it leaves in a sigh.

The rest of the car ride is done in silence.

Turning onto our street, I spot something at the end of my drive.

A For Rent sign.

My heart jumps.

The attached house quickly pulls my eyes away.

Welcome home. It's everywhere.

Seeing the welcome home banners hung across the windows and door, I give in to my tears.

Home.

A wet laugh bubbles out of me. Even the creepy gnome has a sign.

"He still freaks me out," I point out.

"Riley insisted he be included." He grins, climbing out of the car.

My door opens a second after the back passenger door opens and closes.

Taking the cap off, he hands me a water bottle. Pulling out a pill bottle from his inner jacket pocket, Leo shakes two pills into the palm of his hand.

"Take them," he encourages when I shake my head.

"They make me sleepy."

"I know." He nods, but his steely gaze under his dark-rimmed glasses doesn't falter.

I give in.

"We'll go in, and you can take a nap. Samantha and some of the Cromwells are inside, but I'm sure they won't mind waiting a little longer."

What? My heart flutters with love.

"They've been helping empty your house this past week. Everything from your bedroom is now in my house. Our house," he amends. "Everything else, including furniture, has been boxed, labelled, and moved to storage in the Cromwells' trucking office. Christopher assures me that it's safe there. We'll sort through it when you're recovered," he informs me.

"Thank you," I breathe.

Turning, I move my legs out of the car, biting my bottom lip when my shins brush Leo's legs.

Strong hands tilt my head back up. He leans in, brushing his nose along mine and down my cheek.

"You're right, I haven't been touching you. It wasn't because I didn't want to. It was because I couldn't."

My chin wobbles.

"Shhh," he soothes. "I couldn't because I knew the minute that I did, I wouldn't be able to stop. God, I need you."

His words, his tone, and the look in his eyes capture my heart.

"You were struggling before, Shelby."

Before the accident.

"I wanted to give you the time you needed. But this is your home. Right here with me and our girl."

Love and grief choke me.

"We'll talk about everything else later. I need you to get better first."

I nod. I can do that.

"Will you lie with me for a bit?" I ask, climbing out of the Jag.

Leo makes a pain-filled sound, but I know by the look on his face that he won't deny me.

Our steps are small and in sync as we cross the lawn. The small cheer that fills the house as we enter fills my heart.

"My baby," my stepmother calls, pulling me into a tight hug.

"Hi." I sink into her. I've missed her.

I'm passed off to Helen Cromwell.

"And my baby," she whispers, the words just for the two of us.

"Thank you for coming." I hug her tighter.

Soon, the two women who have been a mother to me envelop me together.

"Grrr."

The little growl is accompanied by little hands wedging between our bodies, and then Riley squeezes her whole being into the centre of our trio.

"Hi, Momma."

Curling at the waist, I hug her tight.

"Hi, baby." I kiss her head.

Not wanting to interrupt, my best friend gives me a side hug, kissing my left shoulder.

Standing straight, I groan.

"Okay, that's enough for now." Leonard steps in. "The painkillers should be kicking in any minute. A nap and then she's all yours," he promises the room.

"Aw," Sam and Riley complain together.

"The doctor knows best," Helen's husband says. Christopher cups the back of my head and kisses my forehead softly. "Rest for as long as you need. We'll be here when you wake up. The chocolate cupcakes might not be," he jokingly warns, nodding to his daughter and Riley, who are both eyeing the sweet treats laid out on the kitchen table.

I give a short laugh. "Smuggle one into the cupboard for me."

"Already done." He winks.

I feel Leo's hands on my waist immediately.

"Christopher," he acknowledges.

I try to smother my chuckle unsuccessfully.

"What are you laughing at?" Doc asks, leading me down the hall.

"You," I reply, looking up at him.

He glares playfully. "The only man who gets to wink at you is me."

Slowly lowering onto the bed, I roll my eyes.

"I saw that," he whispers, capturing my chin.

I do it again.

His eyes darken instantly. Tilting my chin, I seek a kiss. My body deflates when the only thing to touch my lip is his thumb.

"Touch me," I plead. I need to know that he still wants me, wants us.

"I am touching you."

This time, my eye roll isn't teasing, nor is my huff.

Tapping his hand away from my face, I kick off my shoes.

"Shelby," he starts.

I shake my head. "Don't worry about it." But the words come out watery.

Reaching for the band of my sweatpants, he tells me, "Lift your hips."

"I got it." I wave him away.

"With what hand?" he challenges, raising a brow. His face quickly softens. "Hey, hey." He captures my cast wrist, placing a kiss on my fingers. "Don't."

I bite my lip.

"I wasn't joking out in the car, Shelby. If I touch you, I won't be able to stop."

I take a sharp breath at his confession.

"I don't want you to stop."

He kisses my fingers again, frowning at the cast. "You need to heal."

"My doctor said I'm okay for that."

"I'm your doctor," he corrects.

"I'm okay, Leo," I whisper.

His eyes drop to my lips.

"I promise. Kiss me."

Doc closes his eyes, looking pained. When his eyes open, he's no longer at war with himself.

"Lift your hips," he orders again.

I do as I'm told. Peeling my sweats off, he takes my socks with them. Gentle fingers untie my sling.

"This goes back on after your nap. I know you sleep better without it, and you need rest."

"Hmm," I hum.

"Those pain pills kicking in?" He grins.

I nod sleepily, my eyes drooping.

"Slowly." He lowers me to the thick pillows.

Opening the bedside drawer to my left, Leo pulls something out. A condom.

"For now, we don't risk it," he explains at my frown.

"You didn't want to before."

Sighing, he brushes my hair away from my face. "You need to heal. We'll talk tomorrow, but I want you to pick a contraception, and I'll sort it out."

My eyes fill at his words.

"Shh."

I close my eyes, feeling his hand slip beneath my black panties.

"You don't want a baby anymore?"

My breath hitches as pleasure builds between my thighs.

"I do." He nods. "But you need to heal. Your body." He presses harder on my clit. "Your mind." He strokes my temple. "Your soul." He leans down to kiss between my covered breasts.

I whimper when his fingers leave me.

Soft kisses rain down the side of my face as he moves above me. The sound of his zipper makes my pussy contract. Thick fingers move my panties to the side.

I've missed this. I've missed him.

"Ahh," I cry out as he enters me.

"Shh." He soothes again.

Leo holds himself above me, his elbows braced on the pillow on either side of my head. We are both soaking in the feel of each other.

Leaning down, he presses his lips to mine at the same time that his hips pull back. He's gentle, slow, and caring as he takes me.

Returning his kiss, I touch my tongue to his.

"I love you," he whispers into my mouth.

My breath catches as he pushes in a little sharper.

"I love you too," I groan, forcing my eyes open.

My body is at war, on the edge of coming, and the pain pills are pulling me under.

The slow rhythm of his body rocking mine aids the medication.

Slipping into darkness, I hear his words whispered into my ear.

"Now this gives me déjà vu." I can hear his smirk.

With my left hand, I flex my fingers on his waist. Leo chuckles above me.

My body's grip on him tightens. Pleasure fills me. My legs shake where they lie on the bed.

Leo chuckles again. "Sleep. Rest," he encourages. "I'll be here when you wake up."

For once, I do as I'm told, letting the feel of soft kisses peppering my collarbone and the gentle rocking of my body soothe me to sleep.

CHAPTER FORTY-SEVEN

Leonard

My phone chimes for the second time, pulling my eyes from the road down to the cup holder where it sits.

Without even looking, I already know who it is.

Helen Cromwell.

I asked her to keep a close eye on Riley while I ran an errand before Shelby woke up. I've had six photos and three videos of Riley and Samantha eating far too much cake already.

Banging in the trunk brings my eyes back to the road. Flipping the turn signal to the right, I turn into the private road leading to the Cromwells' lakeside cabin.

I eye the wooden house. I'd kill to have a house on this lake. It's a shame the Cromwells own it all, but at least Riley will get to enjoy it at summer camp next year.

Throwing the car into Park, I grab my phone. The image that greets me pulls a booming laugh from my chest. Riley is wide-eyed, mouth and cheeks covered in chocolate, my little troublemaker.

I quickly make it my screen saver.

Back to business. Climbing out, I head to the trunk. Releasing the latch, I raise a brow at the man inside.

"Was all that noise necessary?"

Cooper's sweaty face looks up at me, the gag preventing a reply.

Movement from the corner of my eye turns my head. I close the trunk quickly without looking back.

"Doc." Michael nods, stepping off the porch.

Closing the distance, I shake his offered hand.

"How's Shelby?"

I take a deep breath before turning to the youngest Cromwell brother. Kaleb lounges against the porch railing, but his casual slouch doesn't fool me. I know who he is. I have to remind myself that he has his own woman, and his interest in mine is purely a matter of friendship and brotherly love.

Still, irrational or not, the sight of the blond irks me.

"Good. She's resting." I glance at my wristwatch. "I need to get back before she wakes up."

"Is there a reason we weren't invited to the party?" Kaleb asks, straightening. Daniel steps out of the front door, and the wood beneath him groans. Shit, he's huge.

I smirk at Kaleb holding up a finger.

Retreating to the car, I open the trunk again. Reaching in, I grab Cooper by the front of his once blue shirt. Now blood-stained and covered in dirt, it looks like he's been exactly where he was . . . held hostage and tortured for a week.

Cooper stumbles, barely getting his feet beneath him before I'm dragging him toward the house.

The brothers' reaction is instant.

Slapping the wood railing, Kaleb laughs.

Daniel crosses his arms and leans against the front door.

Frowning, Michael joins his brothers on the porch.

Seeing who we're approaching, Cooper digs his feet in and struggles to break free. His eyes scan the yard in pure panic.

My fingers dig into his arms as I tug him up the porch stairs.

"Well, well, well. Would you look at that?" Kaleb grins.

Shoving Cooper in front of me, I kick the back of his right knee, forcing him to his knees. The man grunts as he lands heavily. I snatch the back of his top to stop him from face-planting into the wood since the hands bound behind him are useless to break his fall.

Michael Cromwell steps forward first, assessing Cooper's injured form. "Is he dying?"

"Not yet," I state with a raised brow.

"And what was the point of this?"

"I told your brother that what happened to Shelby was your fault. The three of you should have taken care of him before."

I wait for him to raise his gaze from the man bleeding on his parents' property.

"Shelby is considered your family. She's also my family. Consider this a peace offering. I don't see why we can't co-exist within Cromwell. I'd hate to have to take Shelby away from the only home she's ever known."

Michael purses his lips. Taking a few steps back, he sits in the wicker chair.

"Sam can't lose another best friend," Kaleb tells his brothers.

Michael sighs. "It's no wonder we couldn't find him." He gestures to Cooper. "You had him this whole time?"

I give a casual shrug and tilt my head.

A cell phone chimes. Reaching into his back pocket, Kaleb pulls out his cell. "Jesus." He rolls his eyes.

Daniel grunts, looking at the younger Cromwell.

"Mom sent a picture of Sam. Looks like she's eaten her weight in chocolate. Like that woman needs more sugar."

Daniel smiles, his wide shoulders relaxing.

Michael chuckles from his seat.

Guess I'm not the only one Helen is sending updates to. I glance at my watch again.

"You got somewhere to be?"

I meet Daniel's intrusive stare. "I promised Shelby I'd be there when she wakes up."

Cooper mumbles, the words muffled by his gag.

Stepping around him, I tug the cloth out of his mouth. The knot at the back of his head is tight. He cringes when I pull it over his red and swollen lip to below his chin.

"You want to add something?"

Cooper laughs, but the split lip and blood-soaked temple take any humor out of it. "You really think you can get away with this? You're going to jail, all of you."

Kaleb looks around. "Do you not see where you are, asshole?"

Cooper sobers quickly. "Fuck you!" he hisses. "Do they know that you're screwing their little sister?"

Kaleb reacts immediately, rushing forward, but he's not quick enough. Within three large strides, Daniel crosses the porch.

"You talk too much."

The sound of the sole of his boot connecting with Cooper's chest is something I'll hold dear forever. A crunch that says something is definitely broken.

The bound man flies through the air, his body going over the porch steps and landing in the dirt with a thud.

He coughs, and blood splatters his face.

Michael sighs from his seat.

"No!" Kaleb points at the seated man. "I told you we were done waiting."

Raising his brow, Michael stands. "You're forgetting a witness." He gestures to me.

I place a hand on my chest. "My phone is in my car. If anyone ever finds out, my location will show I was also here. I'm assuming the three of you talked after Kaleb and I did?"

Michael nods.

"I'll stay out of your business if you stay out of mine," I offer. "And just this once, we'll . . . work together."

"And what was your contribution?"

"Other than bringing him here?" I snark. "A broken clavicle, broken wrist, and a reoccurring concussion. It's the least I could do."

"Fair," Daniel acknowledges, tilting his head to me but keeping his body facing Cooper from where he stands at the top of the stairs. "You can go."

When I only blink back at him, the oldest Cromwell expands, "You made a promise. Keeping your word means everything." Meeting my gaze, he gives his own promise. "He'll be dead within an hour."

"Spoilsport," Kaleb whispers from the right of his brother.

Daniel smirks. Reaching into his back pocket, he pulls out a folded knife and holds it out for Kaleb to take.

"See how well he sings without his tongue."

My heart races at Michael's words.

Knowing and seeing are two separate things. The Cromwells and I are two kinds of killers.

"Leave," Daniel's deep tone orders. Stepping back from the stairs, he makes room for Kaleb to pass. The man wastes no time, and neither do I.

I have a family to get back to.

Pained screams and cries follow me to my car, the sound music to my ears in a way I never thought possible.

I'm not this kind of man. I kill quietly, peacefully. But Cooper earned this.

Climbing into my car, I check my cell to see if I missed a call. No. Good, that means my wife-to-be is still sleeping.

Daniel's right. You're only as good as your word.

The Cromwells will keep theirs.

Reversing to the right, I turn the steering wheel to the left, ready to head back the way I came, but I can't and don't stop myself from taking one last look.

The three brothers stand over a bleeding, crying Kyle Cooper while he lies helplessly on the cold ground.

Satisfaction seeps deeply.

He deserves this.

Pressing the gas, I turn the car away, driving to the end of the private road without looking in the rearview mirror.

Turning left, I pull out of the Cromwell drive and

head home, where my two girls wait for me. Shelby changed everything for us.

My future wife, the woman who will be the mother of my children, my neighbor.

Who'd have thought we'd find such happiness in the little town of Cromwell?

EPILOGUE

Leonard

"Doctor, your five o'clock is here." Kathy's voice rings out through my phone.

I frown.

"I don't have a five o'clock," I mutter.

Pulling up my calendar, I frown. I don't have anyone down.

The door to my office opens, revealing my wife. I instantly grin.

"Hi, Dr. Moore."

"Good evening, Mrs. Moore. What can I do for you today?" I ask, playing along.

Shelby bites her bottom lip. "I was hoping to change my birth control."

I frown. "No problem. What method do you want to switch to?"

Looking at me from beneath her lashes, Shelby blushes. "Actually, I was hoping to take it out."

My heart rate spikes. Eyeing her arm where the device is embedded, I round my desk, cupping her face. "Are you sure?" I ask softly.

Taking a deep breath, she nods. "I'm sure," she whispers.

My cock jumps to life.

Grasping her hips, I lift her gently onto my desk and press a soft kiss to her lips. "There's no rush," I remind her.

I'll wait as long as you need.

"I'm ready," she breathes against my lips.

The next time my lips touch hers, it's with bruising strength. Her legs part, allowing me to step between them.

"Do you want to take it out first?" she asks, lifting her arm.

I shake my head, already fighting with my belt buckle. "I can't wait. I need you first."

Her laughter is bubbly and light. Pure, just like she is.

Grasping the back of her neck, I gaze down at her, knowing that I've never loved her more than I do right now and that the same will be true again tomorrow, and the day after that, and the day after that.

The same as it's been for the past two years.

Every day, I fall more and more in love with my wife. The woman who knows every part of my soul and still loves me, even the darkest side.

Shelby is my love, my light, my life.
A lifetime with her isn't enough.

The End.

ABOUT THE AUTHOR

Jennifer Ivy is an author that loves to write dark romance.

The author can be found on several social media sites, such as:

Instagram; jenniferivy_author

TikTok; jennifer_author

Goodreads; Jennifer Ivy

ALSO BY JENNIFER IVY

A Killer's Love

(Series Complete)

Mine

Claim

Taken

Blood

Lock

Killing for Love

Protected